July
Fortnight

For Stu Gourley and Paul Webster.

Also, for my Ella, Noah and Arlo, one day you might understand me

Chapter 1 Less Eligibility

Paninaro by The Pet Shop Boys rattled tinnily out of the cheap Amstrad music centre. The 3-bar graphic equaliser LED lights were constantly in the red and there was a mini Vesuvius in ash upon the black ash coffee table which was strewn with 2 large crystal glass ashtrays and Castlemaine and Skol beer cans.

It was a decent house party; Rob didn't know the girl whose party it was as she went to Alderman Newton's School which was next door to the school Rob went to and he was there by proxy because Reidy and Woodhouse knew her.

The party was in the Glenfield Road area of Leicester which was an affluent area built on the outskirts of the city between the wars with the obligatory double bay windows. This house however was very bare inside with no carpets upon the wooden floors and in need of updating.

The house smelt fusty like an old ladies' fur coats.

Similarly, the party goers were not the affluent type they were from the large council estate called New Parks which was a mile away. New Parks was nothing like the individual, leafy avenues of Glenfield Road and Western Park with their nice gardens. New Parks was a huge sprawling council estate built for the heroes returning from World War Two. Built as a thank you by the newly elected Labour government that ousted the nation's hero, Churchill. There were two types of houses, the preformed concrete boxes and those made from iron.

The houses had all the post war optimism for the working class with indoor hot and cold water, baths, toilets and a front and rear garden. Large rectangles of grass locally called greens were interspersed and planted with a tree. These greens became football pitches with the tree or track suit tops for goal posts. However, some greens have large black burnt patches left over from the huge bonfires that adorn each green every November like Armada beacons. During these autumnal months youths would pile everything into a pyre, mattresses, wooden gates, fences. Rob's Dad secured their wooden front garden gate with strong wire so that it wouldn't be stolen.

When Rob was at school, he had a mock interview by Mr Kent for Gateway Sixth Form College, Mr Kent gave Rob some words of wisdom 'Do not put New Parks Estate on your address on your letter, son'.

All the post war optimism had evolved into a stigma. A stigma of living in a council house. The English class system is still alive and kicking and the stigma and shame of going into the panopticons of misery that were the workhouses now was replaced by the secret shame of living on a council estate. In Scotland they are called schemes which is a direct pragmatic approach because these areas are far from country estates or philanthropy.

To be cynical these estates were built out of optimism but designed by the middle classes for less eligibility. They were nothing like the leafy suburbs and individuality of Western Park they all looked the same, with the same style of doors, metal framed 3mm cheap metal windows and privet hedges.

The middle classes would know exactly where the working class lived, and so would they know their place at the gate of the rich man's castle.

Rob's Dad recalled to him how he can remember the estate being built using Polish prisoners of war as manpower. How the Yanks drove down the new concrete roads in their tanks and as a young boy shouted out 'Have you got a gum chum?' to them and they doled out sticks of chewing gum to the ragtag youngsters.

When the Tories decided to sell off these homes for heroes in the mid-1980s in Right to Buy scheme, the first thing the owners would do is get a new front door to how the world that they were not less eligible and they owned their own house. Jack your Body by Steve Silk Hurley now rattled out of the cheap Amstrad stereo. The track should have a deep bass drive, but the treble sound of the cheap hi-fi vibrated and distorted and filled the party with musac rather than the artists intention of energy.

The only person in the room who seemed remotely interested in the music was Rob Sutton who sat on the sofa nearest the stereo looking through the records and twiddling the graphic equaliser that made no difference whatsoever to the sound. It wasn't Rob's party, in fact Rob didn't know exactly who's party it was. He was only there because he was now mixing with a close group of lads who had went to the school next door to his. Rob's Alderman Newton's mates were all 16 like Rob and he had been part of the group since he was 15.

 It was a sparsely furnished badly decorated double bayed semi house built in the 1930's in the Dane Hills area of Leicester on Glenfield Road. As Rob reached down for his can of Castlemaine 4X Lager he noticed the black ash cheap coffee table full of drink rings, cans of skol and cheap lager and cigarette ash like a Saharan sandstorm. To his right sat Dez, eagerly looking at Dayle who was trying to make a move on a girl dancing drunkenly in the middle of the living room. Dez had found his prey and he was watching Dale's every move ready to pounce with sarcasm at Dayle's failure.

Dez leaned over to Rob and wryly said 'watch this' and he nodded towards Dale. The music had changed to Jermain Jackson's We don't have to take our clothes off and Dale was moving into position. Dayle had straw blonde long hair that hung like it had been permed. He always got things slightly wrong. He had a pink and white Gino Gemelli jumper on tight bleached jeans and white Puma trainers all of which were not quite right for the casual look of 1987. Dale always got things slightly wrong, music, fashion, timing. The girl was loud and drunk, and she had made a show of herself all night. She would use Dayle as another reason to get even more attention. He started to dance by moving his fore arms up and down. Rob turned to Dez and said in hysterical laughter 'He's bloody bell ringing'.

Dez was transfixed he did not acknowledge Rob's statement. However, when Dayle made his move by approaching the girl from behind and putting his arms around her hips. Dez's concentration was broken as she turned around expecting a George Michael and getting Dayle she uttered the word'Urggh'.

Dez erupted with laughter his laugh was a cross between a cackle and a whoop! Dayle looked over and quickly shot Dez the V sign with his fingers which added even more to the comedy moment.

As the music rattled out of the speakers Rob sat on the sofa with his arm around his girlfriend Angela. He had first noticed Ang' when he was bored in his English lesson looking out at the end of the afternoon across the school yard. The tacky school tables from the Porta cabin classroom were cold under Robs elbows as he saw her walk across the school yard on her way home. He'd never noticed her before, she wore a short grey skirt and a cream baseball style jacket, her hair was a short shaven bob at the rear and a dyed blonde with the darker roots showing where it was shaven at the back. Rob remembers that first time that he'd noticed her on that late September afternoon when the sun was still warm and sent a golden glow across the school yard the amber warmth of the autumnal sun gave Rob a happy, melancholic feeling.

Rob noticed her more and more around the schools wooden floored corridors and through windows where she was in lessons. Rob had asked Canky about her one day when they went fishing and he knew exactly who she was. Rob and Canky had decided to go fishing on the Grand Union Canal in Aylestone and had stopped for some crisps and a can of Tango. Rob held the bikes outside at the petrol station and Canky went in to make his purchase.

As Rob stood next to the litter bin someone had left a cooked kipper in newspaper on top of the bin. Rob quickly put the fish in his box. Halfway through the days fishing Rob decided to bring up the topic of Angela. Canky was quick to respond 'You've got to be prepared to shag if you go out with her mate, she's a rider plus She's going out with Alderman Newton's hardest kid though his names Adie Smith, she's been shagging him for years, you'd prob' do him though Rob anyways, I'm off for a Gypsies kiss' and with that Canky went into the bushes.

Whilst he was away Rob wound Canky's line in and attached the cooked kipper to his hook and cast the line back in. The smell of the kipper and Rob's fishing box smelt of Smokey death. Splash as the clumsy rig hit the water, and the float sunk, and the ripples settled just in time.

Things always seemed to happen to Canky. Last year the summer months were often spent knocking a golf ball around over the school fields. Each youth had to have their own club. Rob had a 7-iron made by Ping whilst Canky had his trusty 5 iron. This summer's evening just when the sun was beginning to set Rob and Canky were playing the par 3 from the cricket pitch to the old Elm Tree.

The school fields were bisected by the black pad which led from New Parks through to Western Park. These school fields were the equivalent to the Victorian's release for their population within their new parks. Rob father had sat on his last day of school on these fields back in 1954 and the same thing would happen to Rob by sheer coincidence in 1985.

Canky had taken his shot and walked about 80 metres towards the Elm Tree whilst Rob had a wild wee in the bushes. Rob placed his golf ball upon the castle tee and struck it so cleanly that it flew in a perfect trajectory with purpose. The ball did not draw or fade like most of Rob's shots and he knew that the minute it left his club it was going to hit Canky in the distance.

'Canky!' Rob shouted. Canky looked over his shoulder and saw the ball coming to him like a missile aimed at the Sir Galahad a few years before.

Canky tried to outrun it, but it was no good the ball hit him squarely on the back of his neck, it knocked him in a complete somersault, and he caught the golf ball in the hood of his Nike cagoule. Rob ran up to him and couldn't stop laughing.

Canky returned from the bushes talking and doing up the fly on his jeans." Any ways Rob I'm gonna tell her, she's in my maths class"

"you can do mate, but I don't think she'll know who I am" was Rob's reply secretly pleased because she's known that Rob hung around with popular, funny fashionable lads like Canky.

Canky had a blonde flick head haircut, he wore Farah trousers with the bottom seams cut to sit correct over his Adidas München trainers. He completed his look with a Pringle V neck jumper. When Canky sat back on his box he noticed that float had gone under water. Canky struck by quickly pulling his rod into the air. Always one to overreact he began the running commentary of landing the fish.

'It's a big un, it's making a run for the reeds, Rob get the landing net'. Canky always one to exaggerate was leaning back and struggling making out that he was landing a shark.

After 3 or 4 minutes of playing the dead fish Canky finally caught sight of his catch through the water, with its golden glow. It glowed as if the brief case had been opened by Vincent Vega in Pulp Fiction.

"It's a Golden Orff!" Canky exclaimed. But as the fish was scooped into the landing net. Canky looked confused, Rob burst out laughing, "They're coming out, ready cooked now Canky".

True to his word Canky did tell Angela that Rob liked her and after another month of Rob and Angela looking at each other from afar, lasting looks and glances and as if they had a seventh sense they started noticing each other everywhere, he finally plucked up the courage to ask her out and by Christmas they were a couple and in love.

Canky had done Rob a huge favour putting the wheels in motion and Rob was as nervous as hell when he asked Ang out. They arranged to meet on the night of December 7th at 6-30. Rob lived with his Mam, Dad and Nan and his Mam and Nan left the house at 6 for bingo at the primary school, and Rob put on his best clothes, grey stay pressed trousers, white Fred Perry Polo shirt, grey white and black boating blazer, army parka and bowling shoes. He even splashed on some Hai Karate aftershave that he had been given for Christmas the year before.

Rob's Dad was sitting in his arm chair in the living room reading the Leicester Mercury, Whilst Crossroads was on the television, Benny was stuttering his unrequited love for Miss Dianne and Rob's Dad was pretending not to notice Rob but really he was just as nervous for his son away on his first ever date. His Dad loved his only son. He himself had an awful upbringing during the war. He had stepfathers who had beaten him and his mother and left home at 14. He was strong mentally and physically but a true gentleman. He was the hero worker at the centre of Ford Maddox Brown's painting, Work, with the rose in his mouth. He was a firm believer in the Victorian values of hard work 'I must work the works of him that sent me for the night cometh, wherein no man can work'. He had been commended for bravery as a fireman, yet he was constantly haunted by the experience that he had at Aberfan and now worked beneath his ability in the Co-operative Dairy. Despite being always smartly dressed and groomed and with copious use of carbolic soap Rob's Dad always held the felt smell of stale milk.

Angela walked through the front gate and approached the wooden front door. The December evening was clear and crisp, and frost had already started to settle. She reached up and tapped the bronze pixie door knocker and tapped purposely three times. Rob was already in the hallway but took a couple of moments so that he did not look like he was going to be too keen.

Rob opened the door and smiled. There was no awkwardness. They walked and talked in the cold air. Their walk took them through Gilroe's Cemetery and down to the Victorian factory where Rob's Mam worked. They sat upon the bench in the old tram terminus shelter that was now a bus shelter. The conversation had flowed and as they sat Rob asked politely if he could put his arm around her and she snuggled into his neck like a mammal seeking protection.

Their walked continued through the middle-class area of Letchworth Road with their neat Spruce and Yew tree lined front gardens, lit up with coaching lanterns like a Dickensian Victorian Christmas scene. Rob said that he's live in this area one day. The couple ended up and sat upon a bench behind the council flats. The flats were angular like Bauhaus but more functional than aesthetic, the H block brick school loomed across the field from them. The school and the flats leered at each other like huge brick monolithic leviathans. The frost was so thick that when they sat down the cold passed immediately through their clothes to their bottoms. They chatted about the video to the Band Aid single and Rob obsessed with Weller whilst Angela was more Fun Boy 3 and Nick Heywood. The cold air drifted almost visibly like a spectre across the school field in front of them. They had to move. The night was almost over and the couple walked to Angela's Road. As they said goodnight Rob had his first ever kiss. As they embraced each other on Bird's Nest Avenue, Rob was already in love. He had fallen he couldn't help himself; it was a hope and feeling that he had never felt before, he was free falling, backwards through the air his arms and legs outstretched in front of him, wind whooshing past his ears. Hopefully, he would not stop and get the jolt that happens when he fell when he was sleeping.

It was the best Christmas period that Rob had ever had, Christmas shopping with Ang' on Christmas Eve, Milkshakes at Bruccianis with Last Christmas by Wham being played in the shops , the condensation of the café as they looked at the neon lights of Irish Menswear through the condensation distorted windows. The evening was spent walking the streets and kissing under the Christmas lights placed upon a fir tree on Letchworth Road, and finally in his box room heavy petting took place. Rob's hand slipped under Ang's dungarees top and on to her small breasts, to which she replied as an apology 'You won't find much up there'.

As Rob's hand explored beneath the bottom part of her dungarees and around and inside her cotton knickers, she candidly retorted 'You'll find something down there'. Rob certainly did find something when his fingers toughed the string tail of her tampon and his hand quickly recoiled, and he felt his face heat up and blush.

That was Rob's best Christmas Eve, the anticipation, the hope. All his childhood Christmases were made special by his Mam and Nan who made everything just so despite not having much money.

After he walked Ang home, Rob sat looking out of his box room window into the clear, silent, Christmas Eve night. He listened to Love Reign O'er Me by The Who through his headphones and the synthesizers added to his contentment, he finished his bag of Walker's Smokey Bacon crisps eating them as quietly as he could from their maroon packet and went to sleep.

Three months later the couple were sitting on the sofa at the party. Rob had started hanging around with lads from Alderman Newton's School not his native New Parks School as they were Mods. Mambo came running into the living room with a used condom 'I've done it', he exclaimed. He had just lost his virginity to Rachel Derbyshire. He was so pleased with himself holding his rubber trophy aloft. His nick name was unfortunate as his mam had body odour hence Mambo. This celebration was enough for Rob and Ang' who left the party to return home. Sometime later a contingent of the Leicester Baby Squad, Toogood, Jelly, Troy, Beezer and Riaz and demand that they had 'come for Rob'.

Rob was renowned for being hard, but it was really the legacy of his Dad.

Chapter 2 In between Days

A year later things had revolved completely for Rob. It was the complete loss of hope for the future that made him feel completely hollow inside, a void and pain that he had never felt before, it choked him. His Dad had always been there for him and his advice was always true, 'time's a great healer, things are always better in the morning and as one door closes, another one open's. Of course, these nuggets of wisdom did not help Rob's broken heart. He was haunted by Angela; he saw her on the last bus going into town on a Thursday night whilst he listened to late night feelings of Dexy's Midnight Runners through his headphones looking out of his window whilst the rain drops on the window had races. He saw her spectre in nightclubs, on Western Park, outside places they had been, THEIR places, Rob was torturing himself. He even saw her ghost at Blackpool Pleasure Beach when he went for the weekend organised by Doreen Dirty Nets, his Mam's next-door neighbour. Around every corner she was waiting.

It had been such a good summer, not the Long Hot Style Council Summer that Rob wanted but the couple were still in love. They went on the National Express to London on a hot summer's day. The city was bright with its light bricks of

Regents Street and Piccadilly Circus. They walked and shopped in Carnaby Street at the Cavern and Merc shops. In the afternoon they walked to Green Park and lay on the grass, Rob took his boating blazer off and Ang unbuttoned his light grey and white striped short sleeved shirt to his chest and lay her head upon it in the sunshine. Rob wondered if this was Itchycoo Park?

On the bus journey home Ang lolled contented upon Rob's shoulder with her hand through the buttons on his shirt on his chest.

It's incorrect to think that only rural dwellers notice the change in the seasons. In the city and suburbs, the people notice how quickly the nights draw in, how the flying ants leave the cracks in the pavement to signal the end of summer. The streetlights coming on earlier and the noise of the kids walking the pavements in their throngs returning to school. All signals that summer is over city dwellers. Rob's romance was also dead like summer.

Rob felt that he'd lost everything, Angela, his place in the world at New Park's School. His school friends like Wardy and Canky, he'd stopped doing his A/levels in History and English at Gateway College as he spent more and more time skiving and drinking in the Rutland and Derby Arms, eventually they had to kick him out of college. Rob now worked as a trainee manager for Ratner's the Jewellers in Leicester's Silver Arcade. He hated it. He had lost contact with Wardy. Sam Ward was his closest school friend. Rob had gone on holiday with Wardy's family to Alcúdia when he was 14. It was a huge revelation, flying, different culture and food and different family rules, freedom. Rob's Dad never took him on holiday because of his alcoholism and agoraphobia yet he loved Rob despite being a Victorian Dad.

In Alcúdia the cross over from boys to men was transitioning. The lads had taken fishing rods and one day in the hot sun they were fishing with cheese as bait in Porto Pollensa Harbour. Rob cast his line out and it got snagged for the tenth time on the rocks behind so with frustration he yanked and yanked.

Rob heard a noise 'aghh'. As he turned Wardy had both hands in front of his face. 'My eye, my eye!' Rob managed to pull Wardy's hands away and he had hooked him through the right eyebrow and the huge lump of cheese was still attached to the hook. The huge yellow cuboid of protein was a new growth on Wardy's face. Rob could not stop laughing as he unhooked Wardy, who was still in shock trying to explain how he had felt the line whip across his bare chest.

Two girls from Plymouth had been interested in Wardy and Rob on the holiday and for the first time Rob had had a proper drink, ice cold San Miguel's that had a bitter, malty taste. Now the lads looked around shops for Lacoste polo shirts not toys and Rob read his first book, Christine by Stephen King that he had been given by Sally, Wardy's sister, he related to the characters also at the same stage of life as himself.

The smell, the golden light of a new country was all new to Rob and he sponged it all in. He missed the tranquillity of solitude and often went for a walk on his own, content with his own thoughts for half an hour before returning to Wardy.

The adolescence changes in the book seemed to mirror Rob's changes. Things were somehow different when they returned to England but nowhere as different and alien as the past 12 months.

As one door closes another one opens, this was certainly true regarding Rob's new friends. So much had changed, he'd lost contact with his Alderman Newton's Mod Friends Woodhouse and Reidy as they continued with their A/Level Politics and he had a new group of friends by association to Woodhouse.

Dez was the closest of Rob's new friends. He was small, stocky and game for anything and to experience anything. He came from a single parent family and he was as hard as Leicester slate. Dez had a wedge haircut that made his head look like a mushroom. Dez had started an apprenticeship with Jones and Shipman Engineering. As an initiation some of the older guys at work had got two metal cuffs and placed them over Dez's wrists and tried to weld him to the metal tabletop. Dez had moved and the hotel metal burnt his wrists, he had now 2 opal fruit shaped welt burns on the top of his wrists forever. Dez did not cry or complain.

Steve was Dez's oldest friend. They both had Geordie parents. Steve was athletic but, had a scar across his chest from a childhood operation. Steve was also game for anything, scared of nothing and a loyal friend who was an apprentice painter and decorator.

By proxy Boon was added to the group. He was the World's angriest man. The same age as the others but a renowned football hooligan. Boon dressed well and clothes always looked good on him despite his small stature he oozed confidence and respect. Steve had met up at Charles Keen College where they both went one day a week as part of their Youth Training Scheme. Boon had attitude and style. He had a mushroom perm haircut and his casual clothes hung right. In his first job working as an apprentice painter and decorator for the council he refused to sit in the back of the van. Simply, snarling and pushing the button of the locking van door down when the time served 55 years old man tried to enter the van in the shotgun seat.

The final friend was Dayle. He was different to the other lads. He never got it quite right. He had long light blonde hair which hung in curls and looked like a perm. He had a hook nose and was often called Jasper as an insult in his resemblance to the comedian Jasper Carrot. Dayle was the youngest son to elderly estranged parents and had older brothers and sisters who were 20 years his senior. Dayle did have a heart of gold. All the lads followed the underground soccer casual fashion with brands such as Sergio Tacchini, Lacoste, Fila, Chevignon, Benetton, Pringle and Best Company.

However, Dayle never looked right, he wore Farah's that were a shade of brown that had never been seen before and often combined with a pastel blue and pink Gino Gemelli v- necked jumper. Even Rob had put away his parka and Mod clothes and adopted casual fashion.

This in between pre-pub age was awkward at times. They were 17 years old and it was late summer. The lads still met on Sundays on Western Park. Weggy Park was special to Rob, it's one of his first memories. When he was five years old Rob's Dad had taken him over to the park on a summer's evening. Rob remembers walking up the black path between the school fields and holding his Dad's huge square hands. His Father pointing things out to Rob. After the slides and swings. Their walk back took them past a huge old oak tree. Rob's Dad gave Rob a stick and told him to hit the tree three times and run as a giant lived up the great tree. Rob did this, 'thwack, thwack, thwack' and they both ran laughing and looking back expecting the giant to jump from the broad leaves.

Over a decade later Rob was sitting under the tree with his mates. They had been kicking a football about for a while before it had gone into the paddling pool and they had ended up splashing each other before they had all turned on Dayle and soaked him. These were the in between days.

Dez had bought a motorbike. It was a cheap Yamaha FZ 50 a fizzy. The engine looked tiny sitting in the frame. It was like Michelangelo's David with its small appendage. Rob asked if he could give Steve a croggy, [a pillion] ride through the park on it. Dez threw the keys over and Rob caught them like Ian Botham in the slips at Grace Road.

Rob and Steve got on the bike and the tiny two stroke spurted into life and the two of them sped off at ten miles an hour leaving a mist of acrid smelling white smoke and the noise of a bumble bee caught in a jam jar. When they got to the end of the road that weaved its way through the park Rob stopped the machine and suggested to Steve that for a laugh, they should ride back naked.

It was at 3 pm that sunny afternoon that Dez turned around to see his new motor bike being ridden by two naked, pale while teenagers laughing their heads off. Dez was non plussed when the two lads pulled up, but the other lads could not stop laughing as they bent over pointing. 'Steve your dick's like a frazzled sausage mate' Boon spurted out. 'I hope there's no skiddies on my seat 'Dez added.

It was an awkward age. Rob worked in a Jewellers, but he got every forth Saturday off. Those Saturday's were spent going down the football. Meeting up with Jonny, Angelo, Barrell and the other Knighton Young Baby Squad. The lads would shout abuse at the away fans who were in police escorts and hung around the warren of terraced streets and the Royal Infirmary hoping for a fight, which rarely happened. The lads would always go into the middle pen in the Spion Cop in Filbert Street. Jonny said that Pen 1 near the away supporters was for 'king divs'.

Football had become a big part of Rob's life. It had shown him other parts of England. In 1981 he went away to watch Leicester versus Oldham Athletic. It was the first time that he had seen the satanic mills and grey streets of the North West. It was also the first time he saw a lady's thigh as Oldham had Bunny Girls on the pitch before the game.

More recently Rob with his new understanding of local rivalries [possibly a for runner of the old Elizabethan Parish system and beating of the bounds] got involved in the fighting.

He went to Leyton Orient away with Dez and the Steamers on a coach. The Steamers were men who mostly worked on Leicester Market in their 30s and 40s. They were hard working, hard drinking, hard men. In London the bus was stoned by Chelsea fans, the Steamers wasted no time in getting off the bus and laying into the youngsters, Rob loved the buzz and managed to give a young Chelsea fan with a Burberry scarf around his nose a bloody nose.

One afternoon Boon, Rob and Johnny decided to wait upon the railway platform at Leicester for the arriving QPR football special. The train arrived and as the doors flung open a meant and ear-splitting chorus of 'We hate Leicester' deafened the lads. The soundwaves reverberated and echoed around the old timbers and structure of the Victorian station raising the ghosts from their slumbers.

That was enough and the three lads were scared and quickly evacuated the Victorian stairs that John Merrick had once walked. At the top of the Stairs the three lads saw some other Squaddies waiting to welcome the Ranger's fans. It was Riaz, Suff and a small crew of the Melton Road, St Matthew's Squad. As they walked past them, they noticed that they had the same idea and exited the station and walked down London Road away towards the city centre. Leicester was is a multi-cultural city and there have never been any real problems with racism. After the war Indians were encouraged to move to Leicester and saved its failing hosiery industry. During the partition some Pakistanis also settled in the city and there was also a small Caribbean community in the Highfields area. Indeed, Leicester's top boy was black.

The Baby Squad was not one homogenous unit it was made up of separate groups of lads from different suburbs and areas of the city with a common cause. Some groups were loosely affiliated like the Wongs and even though there was no racism in the Squad there was elitism mostly exerted by the hanger's on. Once and older lad known as The Mole, who was used for finding information about movements other groups walked past Rob, Steve and Boon in Yates' Bar on a Saturday afternoon.

He went to the toilet and then returned to square up to Rob. 'What's up, do you wanna picture? Is it ok that I go to the bogs is it?' he said aggressively. Rob must have looked at him.

'Sorry mate I didn't realise that I stared at you'. The Mole just swaggered off, pleased with himself. Boon said, 'You should have sparked him out mate'. Rob regretted that he had not.

The swagger that the Mole had, and patronising rudeness was apparent in some other Squad lads. Funde who Rob had gone to school with, played rugby with and grew up with, spoke out of the side of his mouth when he was with the Funk Crew.

Rob was sensitive for a big lad and he tried to hide it. He often thought too deeply about things and not deeply enough about others. Steve said that he had no common sense. Rob was certainly a victim of trying to live up to the image that he thought people thought of him. A type of Simone de Beauvoir affliction that's suggested in her book, She Came to Stay.

The Boy about Town song played in his head every day as he walked through the city centre with his Head bag slung over his shoulder on his way to work.

Going to the football was multi-faceted. It was fashion, friends, music and kudos. There was also laughs and far less fighting than publicised, it was mostly running in Rob's case. One funny outrageous moment was when Leicester were at home to Shrewsbury Town in the F.A Cup. There was a break in the game and out from the crowd ran one of the Steamers, Ant Reed. He had full Leicester City home kit on and a ball. He ran in front of the home crowd in the Spion Kop and took a penalty against a non-plussed Shrewsbury keeper.

The Saturdays that Rob worked he would often meet Steve for a drink at lunch in the Pinch of Snuff Pub on Church Gate, a haunt of the Baby Squad. Rob would order vodka and orange as his manager Tony the Perv' would not smell booze on his breath, A shot of Vodka, and an inch of room temperature orange cordial, tasted tart and horrible. Indigestion time bomb.

It was the late Autumn of that year that Rob passed his driving test. The next day his Dad took him to pick up the orange Ford Escort Mark 2 that he had bought for him for £420. Rob loved it, it was only a 1.1 basic model, Rob soon made it his own with a furry steering wheel cover and a stuck on you Garfield cat in the back window. He also put Benetton stickers on each front wing, but his Dad soon took them off disapprovingly.

It was Friday night and Rob were going to pick his mates up in his new car and go to some new pubs. They started off at the Red Cow in Leicester Forest East, a pub with a thatched roof that was busy and had a mixed crowd in.

After a couple of pints with no problem getting served, they headed out into the verdant Leicestershire countryside. Through the patchwork of hedges and village greens, the sun setting on the late autumnal evening casting long shadows as the orange machine made its way like a time machine through the enclosure award set square hedges to the Bull's Inn pub at Woodhouse Eves, a very 'des-res' thatched village that the council estate lads had only seen in books and pictures. It was alleged that the England Goalkeeper Peter Shilton lived there.

It was agreed that the evening was to end back at the Red Cow Pub as there were more 'birds' in there. The lads were well oiled by the neck oil on the drive back and Dez put a cassette into the player and the starting notes of the A chord of Pretty Vacant rang out before the lads went crazy singing and wrecking inside the car, making it difficult for Rob to drive.

The lads were in fine spirits as the car pulled into the large car park and they entered the pub once more, which was now full of young people. Their noses once again filled with the stale smell of hops and their eyes widened by the golden glow of their lagers. Their ears rang with a hundred indistinguishable voices. They stood in a circle with their drinks laughing and Rob had his designated driver soft drink of choice, a tomato juice with Worcestershire Sauce.

As fast as lightening the mood changed. B just said two words 'trouble, trouble'. Steve said to Rob, 'those lads there are staring at us'. Rob immediately looked over, which was the wrong thing to do. When the snake stalks its prey. The rabbit does not see the stealthy reptile. The moment that the rabbit stops eating and looks up sensing the snake, the serpent will strike the rabbit.

The game was up, the hunters knew that the hunted knew that they were the prey. The lads thought that the best decision was to leave. Rob left first at the head of the group followed by the others. Dayle was the last of the door and barely through it before Southy a lanky, blonde haired lad spoke to him. 'oi you have you been round here snapping car aerials?' Dayle replied 'no mate'.

Southy replied 'yes you fucking have you lying bastard!'

Dayle's next words were 'run lads!' with that he was away running as quickly as he could down the Hinckley Road. From this point on Dayle was referred to as rabbit for running off, a derogatory term that he didn't truly deserve. Eleven lads piled out of the pub, they were older and much bigger, men not boys. Steve and Boon got into minor scuffles on the roadside but escaped.

Dez had ran down a cul-de-sac chased by three predators. He turned to face his fate. Biffo a huge man and an accomplished kick boxer set about unleashing punches on Dez's head in quick combinations. The other two joined in kicking Dez. A warm feeling ran down Dez's face, it was blood. He was cut above his left eye. Every time the blows reigned down Dez said 'is that all you've fucking got?' Biffo was not angered by this, he actually respected Dez and stopped hitting him. Eventually, Biffo asked after his wellbeing 'Are you alright mate? You did well there'

'Fuck off' was Dez's reply, 'get lost'. The aggressors walked with him to the top of the cul de sac and tried to make sure that he was ok. Dez's face was now tight and sore, he constantly refused help from his assailants in this strange Stockholm Syndrome incident.

Rob had calmly walked back to his car and got in without being accosted. He could have turned and fought or helped his friends but for some reason he didn't instead he got into his car and reversed it by mistake into the pub wall.

Rob now picked his friends up one by one. A furious Dez firstly refused to get into the car, angry for being left alone to fight. 'Fuck off! He repeatedly shouted angrily. When he finally did the car was in silence, no one speaking. Rob was embarrassed by his guilt of not helping his friends. They returned to Rob's house and Rob's Mam and Dad cleaned Dez's eye under the strong white glare of the fluorescent kitchen strip light. The TCP stung and Rob's Dad insisted upon holding smelling salts under Dez's nose.

On Monday after Steve and Boon had been on day release to Charles Keen College, they met up with Rob to tell him the news. 'Rob you know Kirky?' Well he knows the lads that got us. He lives with one of them a big fucker called Biffo'

Kirky was a painter and decorator also on a Youth Training Scheme that Boon and Steve had become friends with. Kirky was a good lad, salt of the Earth and trustworthy.

'He says to leave it mate. They know that they got the wrong lads.

Rob trusted this advice he had met Kirky once. Picking him up with Steve outside the Merry Monarch pub in his orange escort. They had gone for beers in

Cropston, out into the countryside. The inner-city poor lads driving through the enclosed fields that were naturally, unnatural, made by men planting hedges on instructions of higher-class men making the eighteenth-century enclosure awards taking land off the rural poor lads two centuries before.

Rob automatically liked Kirky. He was naturally friendly and a great raconteur. He spoke using rhyming slang, referring to the pain in his 'union Jack' after bending down all day. He had long cow eyelashes and was thick set and a good boxer.

Call it fate or predestination, free will or Plato's shadows in the cave but the lads and men who had fought with Dez and Steve, ended up being part of their extended friendship group, thanks largely to Kirky being friends and Dez's resilience.

Later that night the lads were round Dayle's house. His front room always had his Mum and Aunt sitting in there smoking and putting the world to rights whilst watching the soaps. They stubbed their cigarettes out in ash trays that stood on stalks like Triffids and were rarely emptied, the whole hose smelt of stale smoke.

The lads were in Dayle's bedroom, Steve was sat upon the bed looking at Dayle's 10-year-old porn mags' which were full of girls in woolly striped stockings and had names like Razzle. These sorts of magazines were always found hidden or discarded in bushes, they were as common as white dog shit.

'I prefer the over 50s Readers' Wives' Steve said, 'More realistic to who I would pull'.

Rob and Boon were playing with Dayle's vintage Bull Worker when, 'Smash!'

The sound echoed around the room and time seemed to stop. Rob had been holding the Bull worker like a bow and arrow, as if he was at Agincourt or Bosworth Field. It was a strange piece of body building equipment; it had a hydraulic pipe to push or two strings to pull. Rob was pulling the strings as hard as he could and had let go by mistake and the whole thing had flown out of his hands and crashed out through the first story 3mm window with its cheap metal frames and onto the garden path below.

'Dayle!!!!!!!!!!!!!!'

Chapter 3 The Queen Is Dead

Christmas was fast approaching, and Rob's shop had employed twelve female Christmas staff. Tony the Perve had interviewed them all and his first sift was to dispose of any men, ladies over 30 and foreign names in their letters of application. After the loneliness and the in between Christmas of last year the build up to the festivities were a good time for Rob.

Christmas music in the shop, new staff, nights out and happy festive customers. The shop stood on the edge of the ancient market and the corner of a Victorian arcade thus adding to the Yule tide ambience.

There was a downside to Christmas at the shop. On Christmas Eve, Tony let some of the staff go earlier, just leaving five female staff and himself, Sweaty Nigel [the assistant manager] and Rob. Tony dead locked the door and said to the girls 'you can all go if you give us a Christmas snog'. His horrible carrot ginger balding, greasy hair with its flapping, thinning fringe hovering above his weedy silver framed square glasses.

Rob felt uncomfortable and after a pause which seemed to last an Ice Age said pleadingly 'C'mon Tone let them go, they will miss their busses'.

Tony realising that he was caught in a quandary quickly changed into a jovial, joking, chappy, dancing from one foot to the other.' Only joking ladies have a great Christmas, thanks for all your hard work', and with that her opened the door with a broad smile upon his slimy pale face.

When they had left, he turned with a face of pure malevolence realising that his chance of touching a female other than his downtrodden wife had gone.

He stormed up to Rob grabbling Rob's tie and pushing it up to his throat and his candy-striped shirt. 'Do you want this fucking job or not?' Tony said as he spoke his spittle came out like a spitting Cobra. Rob did not know what to do, he could fill Tony in, no problem but then he wouldn't have a job.

'I was just trying to help out Mr Bates, I thought it was getting awkward and they wanted to go'.

Tony released his grip and said, 'Never undermine me again, you understand?'.

With that the Jekyll and Hyde character of Tony the Perv Bates changed back to the jovial happy chappy and pulled out two envelopes stuffed with cash.

'Christmas bonus boys. He said through his smile and gave Rob and Nigel their brown envelopes.

On Boxing day with his £200 Christmas bonus Rob went shopping. He bought a pair of black Lois corduroy trousers and a pair of baby blue Adidas gazelle trainers.

It was just after Christmas that one of the Christmas girls asked Rob out. He knew that he didn't really like her but, it was something to do and a bit of female interaction after Angela and a brief fling with Karen Tulloch a Scottish Modette that he'd met at a Makin' Time concert at Leicester University Students' Union and most of their dates were spent on the Banks of the Grand Union Canal or in the Crow's Nest Pub.

Jane Onions was on a gap year from Oxford University. Her Dad was a headmaster at a large secondary school in Hinckley. They lived in a huge detached house on Lutterworth Road and its Edwardian grandness stood back powerfully from the main road approached from an in and out drive. Rob didn't really fancy Jane she was just something to do, an inbetweener. The two main things he did like about her were the Lacoste Polo shirts that she wore and her very large breasts.

Rob would date Jane in the week. He would go around her house and she would cook his tea and the huge cockatoo would squawk and go mental trying to get food. Rob started denying food at Jane's because of the bird. Jane's family was away skiing, and Rob would end up kissing on the sofa until the early hours his hands would be allowed up Jane's Lacoste Polo Shirt to the reward of her very large but soft with their small nipples.

Their other weeks would be mid- week either to the Bulls Head at Woodhouse Eves or the Haunch of Venison on the High Street in Leicester. Each date would usually end up in the countryside car parks of Swithland Woods where more mammary massaging ensued.

Rob never saw Jane at weekends this time was reserved for his mates. The lads were now all confident in drinking downtown. Friday's and Saturday's followed the same route. The Griffin, The Tavern upstairs to the Bohemian, up the stairs to Rickshaws and then either to Legends Nightclub to drink and listen to music that was funky like Shannon's

Let the Music play or Jermaine Stewarts We Don't Have To.

The other option was the Superbowl Nightclub that played the new house music from Chicago and the lads Jacked their body on the dancefloor to tunes such as Love Can't Turn Around by Farley Jackmaster Funk. Steve would piss himself laughing at Rob's dancing with his Christian Dior blazer off his shoulder revealing his candy-striped shirt. Similarly, Dayle's dancing was like a giant spider with arms and legs stretched out. There was also Dayle's pulling dance which looked like he was ringing hand bells before her went in and grabbed the girl in a Gypsy style grabbing move from behind. This was never successful.

Sunday afternoons would be spent kicking a ball around in Bradgate Park, with Steve acting out scenes from Rambo in the trees in the avenued Tudor deer park. All the lads met at Dez's house by tradition and he was often in his room with the House martins or Small Town Boy by Bronski Beat blaring out through the fabric of the house.

The lads were now a close-knit group that spent lots of time together. There were links with larger outlying groups of friends but the five were a solid core. Crazy winter nights were spent driving around the country lanes, Rob would turn the lights to side lights and say that they were in a spaceship or a tipsy Steve or Dez would lie on the car bonnet as a dare as Rob sped along.

One-night Rob agreed with Steve to pick Kirky up and help them steal some fencing. Kirky had bought a Dobermann Pincer dog and he could not keep it from jumping over his garden fence. His idea was to go to Groby Community College in the dark and cut a section of the school fence down with bolt croppers and reassemble in his back garden.

The three lads arrived in the dark at the end of the school field. Rob kept watch whilst Kirky cut through the green plastic covered wire fence. He cut up vertically for about six feet and then horizontally for about twenty feet whilst Steve supported the weight.

After about 6 feet the weight was tremendous, and Steve just let it drop. When Kirky had finished cutting his huge hole, the three lads rolled it up like a giant's string vest. The idea was to strap it to the roof of the escort but no matter how hard they tried they could not lift the fence! Rob was trying his hardest but Steve and Kirky were falling about laughing 'ow mi union Jack', we aint never gonna move this sausage,' and the great hoist was abandoned.

Kirky's dog was called Rexy. It was a black and white Collie and it was as bright as a button. The Postman used to antagonise it by pulling faces at it through the window and dummying putting the post through the letter box. Rexy hated the Postman. The Posty knew Rexy couldn't get out so one day as he came whistling down the garden path, he thought he'd growl at Rexy. Unbeknown to the Postman Rexy was upstairs and there was a window open. As the Posty walked beneath, Rexy jumped out of the window landing on the Posty's shoulders. The Posty stumbled forward like a newly born calf, landed on his knees and in one movement sprang over next doors fence to safety, leaving Rexy on the other side. The Posty was sure Rexy was laughing.

The next time that they saw Kirky was on the following Saturday. Rob had the day off and Boon, Steve, Dez and Rob intended to go down the football, Leicester were playing Middlesboro.

The lads walked into the alternative Helsinki Bar on Regent Street. It was a sunny March early afternoon and the Blue Monday bassline was thumping through the art deco styled bar with its exposed wooden floors and school chairs. The bar was a strange mix of wannabe Robert Smiths with back combed hair, trendy students and casuals. Kirky was sitting there on a wooden school chair with some of the lads that had attacked them a year earlier; Southy, Nellie, Kaff and Biffo. They all shook hands. Boys had become men. On the walk past Leicester Royal Infirmary and through the terraced streets that led to Filbert Street, the pavements were full. Southy walked on the road and a policeman spoiling for a fight said 'ohhh hardman, what's it like to be a dick?' to Southy as he passed by, Southy coolly retorted 'you should know mate', and carried on walking.

Outside the ground they lost Biffo, Nellie and Zaff and turned the corner to see the Middlesboro fans being led in a Police escort. The lads rushed up to them hurling abuse and waving £20 notes, alluding to the fact that the north east of England had unemployment problems since the subduing of the miners by Thatcher.

The Police made a charge and the lads ran up Grasmere Street, a Police horse cornered Rob and its rear quarter pushed him into the wall of a terraced house. Rob smelt the horse s and sweat and the Copper on the horse repeated said' not so tough now then are you ginger'. He hit Rob about three times with his baton and then galloped off shouting' Fuck off now ginger cunt!'

Dez was the unluckiest man alive at the football. Against Portsmouth away he was arrested after a rumble with the Pompey lads for drunk and disorderly. Rob drove to Watford away with Jonny Sutton, Mick Arnett and the Glenny lad Stu Grey. After the game they went to pub in Watford. Rob went to the toilet. When he returned Dez had been fighting with Leicester lads because Watford did not have any lads. Unlucky Dez at a Sex Pistols gig in Hyde Park even lost his Adidas Jeans trainers as he jumped up pogoing and the lad behind stood on his heels and Dez jumped straight out of his shoes, losing them. Unlucky Dez.

Things were changing and Rob had been asked to go and work in Sheffield. It was now early spring, and the winter months of the new year had been good times for the group of friends. Rob's 18th had been eventful. The lads had gone out on the Saturday night and ended up in Granny's Nightclub on London Road. Dayle was on the dancefloor doing his bell ringing moves and the pay £5 and drink all you can entry fee was turning messy.

Dez had already had a tactical sick in the Royal Oak earlier in the night so that he could carry on drinking. It was reminiscent of a Roman vomitorium. Rob was drinking the awful flat Hoffmeister Beer in the run-down upstairs nightclub. He went to the toilet and the room was spinning. Rob puked into the sink. There was vomit filling the sink. Rob added water to try and wash it down the plughole, but the spew was too thick. Yellow with meat and vegetables mixed in.

Steve appeared and announced, 'I'll sort it mate'. With that he put his hands into the sink forcing Rob's vomit through the plughole with his fingers. Rob got home to the spinning bed syndrome, happy birthday. In the morning there was a multi coloured puddle waiting for him. Rob blamed salt and lemon from his newfound love, the Doner Kebab which he could still taste in his mouth.

Steve's birthday was similar he was so drunk that Rob and Dez had to carry him out of the taxi and across the green to his house. Carrying the wounded soldier across no man's land was a challenge and they sat Steve down under the tree in the middle of the green.

'What shall we do Dez?' Rob said concerned. 'Steve's old man will go mental at us'

Steve's Dad was a big Geordie, he had attended a tough borstal school in Blyth in Northern England, and he was a man's man. He referred to Steve's mates as 'Beano characters. He said 'None have real names! Boon, Biffo, Cog!'

Dez said 'Let's leave him under the tree, knock on the door and leg it'. So that's what the lads did.

Steve's Dad didn't hear the door but just before he went to bed he looked out of the window and saw the figure under the tree.

'Quick, Ha'way Jill there's a gadgie under the tree deed call an ammm balance, the Police".

Steve's mam appeared at the window 'Ehh it's our Steven'.

It was the Sunday evening before Rob had to leave for Sheffield for the month and the lads had decided to go to the Odeon Cinema in town to see Crocodile Dundee.

At the pay booth sat a young lady of about twenty years. Dayle lent across the counter, rested upon his elbow, pulled up his sleeve to reveal his Bolex Pub mariner watch and said, 'One for the Croc, love'.

'You what?' was her reply and Dayle quickly said half embarrassed, 'One for Crocodile Dundee please, Mi Duck'. Of course, Dez couldn't stop sniggering at this and Dayle through him the customary V sign.

There was a trailer before the film started. Unusually it was a music video by a band. Rob sat awestruck as he watched the promo video to The Queen is Dead by the Smiths. The drums, the feedback and riffs of Jonny Marr's guitar, the hurtful, vulnerable voice and lyrics of Morrissey. Rob was hooked he had to buy it. The feedback of Jonny Marr's Rickenbacker 360 chimed back to Rob's Modism, Morrissey's lyrics that say everything about my life, changed things. True to his feelings, the first thing Rob did upon his arrival into Sheffield was to call in to a record shop and buy The Queen id Dead and Strangeways Here We Come, on cassette.

Rob was in the north again. Things were different. It's surprising how the payees change so quickly in England, from Wold to moor, Woodland to plain in the blink of an eye. In Spain or America, the payee runs for vast distances without change. With change of payee comes change of accent, a new tribe and Rob quite liked the South Yorkshire vowel pronunciations of the people that greeted him at the shop on Far Gate.

After a day at work, a lad from the shop called Billy took Rob to his Hotel. Billy was a nice lad into the same casual fashion as Rob and the pair warmed to each other. The hotel was in the Nether

Edge area near a large cemetery. Once settled in Rob walked to the red phone box near the graveyard to call home, before retiring to the night and listening and learning from the Smiths.

The month passed uneventfully. Billy had taken Rob out with his friends on Saturday nights into Sheffield. They had gone to bars and to a club called Cairo Jacks and Rob was grateful for the friendship and sadly never saw Billy again after his return to Leicester. Every lunchtime Rob had his lunch in the staff room. There was a pile of holiday brochures and Rob flicked through them in boredom. He looked at the sun kissed beaches, the pools, the tourists in their swimwear and the cost. Then the thought hit him like a thunderbolt, he had the idea that the lads and him should book a summer holiday, that was it, the light was on, Rob went out and called Steve and Steve put the word out and they were due to meet at Rob's the Sunday afternoon that he returned from Sheffield.

Chapter 3 Booking

Rob returned from Sheffield on the train on a sunny, early Spring afternoon. He had decided to ring Jane that night and end things, it was the most humane thing to do. Rob's Mam and Dad were pleased to see him, and he had a chip salad tea.

After tea Rob plucked up the courage to ring Jane and he gave the it's me not you excuse. She did not buy it and cried on the phone. Rob felt guilty. He walked to the back door in the kitchen where his Dad crouched looking out into the garden and smoking a Park Drive cigarette.

There had been a spring shower and the rain had freshened everything up. The World smelt fresh and new and the guilt lifted from Rob and changed to optimism. A Blackbird warbled its lovely tune from somewhere in the large Leylandii trees at the bottom of the garden. Rob's Dad took a large draw upon his cigarette and looking into the middle distance towards the Elm and Willow trees in Stan and Sheila's garden said through the smell of the salt peter 'are you ok son? Breaking up is never easy'. He then continued to tell Rob about his first girlfriend also called Jane and how she could have been Rob's Mother. Rob felt uncomfortable but appreciated his Dad's sentiment.

Sunday teatime came and Dez had picked the lads up in his car. He had passed his driving test and bought an old Austin Allegro car that he called Errol. Rob opened the front door and Dez, Steve, Boon and Dayle entered. They had also brought Phillips who was in two minds about coming on the holiday.

Phillips was a black lad, powerful and muscular. A very good footballer who had been on Aston Villa's and Nottingham Forest's books. He had just been released from Preston North End where he was on a YTS contract. Rob and Dez went to watch him play once at Preston. The manager signalled to substitute Phillips in the second half, but Phillips looked scornfully at him and refused to come off! The manager gave up in the end and the assistant coach put the sign down and Phillips played on. After the game Phillips introduced them to another black player called Mel Toto who had a party trick of wind milling his huge penis as he sat on the side of the bath after the match.

Phillips never really had any intention of going on the holiday but had come along for something to do. In fact, that's when the lads only ever saw him, when he had nothing better to do. Rob liked him and he can remember being proud of Phillips as the pair walked through Leicester and Phillips would stare out any Skinheads. Rob hated Skinheads too. They had made his life a misery as a Mod and the juxtaposition between Caribbean, Windrush and Trojan influence and 80's racism annoyed Rob.

The lads sat in Rob's breakfast room and Rob pulled the sliding doors shut so his Dad and Nan could watch Bullseye and Antiques Roadshow in peace. Rob's Mam had prepared chees and onion and cheese salad cobs which were put upon the table. She took drinks orders with Rob and Dez having Tea and the rest Co-op orange cordial. Steve never drink Tea or Coffee.

The room had anaglypta wallpaper and two paintings on opposite walls facing each other, both by Mr Lynch. The Crying Boy faced a woman who looked like she was from the Amazon Rain Forest standing seductively beside a tree. As a child Rob used to pop the anaglypta bubbles in his Mam and Dad's bedroom before they had it woodchipped. In the corner of the room was a walnut radiogram. Rob's Dad had used to play his Buddy Holly and Glen Campbell records on its years ago. On top of the radiogram was a brandy glass with a cat clinging on the edge and a comedy mouse in the bottom. The glass was flanked by two blue and orange glass fish.

In the centre of the table Rob had bought a pile of travel brochures back from Sheffield. Rob chaired the meeting and he had 3 points on his agenda. Where to go? Price? To go to cover a weekend and do they need entertainment at the hotel? The lads flicked through the brochures; they were all quiet except for Dayle making 'Pwhoar' noises as he looked at the ladies in swimming costumes. 'Look at the Bristol's on her'

Rob began 'Right lads Wardy and Vickers are going to Magaluf, but I think it's too pricey and we ain't got time to save. Kris and Cog are going to Faliraki, but I don't think that it will be busy enough for us. Don't laugh boys but I'm thinking Benidorm!'

'I went a few times when I was a kid' Boon piped up. 'I think it's a good idea'. The other lads nodded in agreement.

Rob continued, 'I think that we should book so it includes a weekend so we can go to a club like. Also, if we go July Fortnight it will be busier'.

When Britain was a manufacturing, industrial nation different specialising cities had factory close downs certain fortnights or weeks in the summer. Leicester's was the first two weeks of July. Even the schools finish their summer terms earlier in Leicester to accommodate this.

'I've found this place in the Thompson Book, it's called the Bruno's Aries Apartments and it's just £165 for two weeks, we also get £5 deposit and free insurance if we book with Lewis's.'

With that Rob passed the two copies of the brochure around showing the huge 25 floor tower block at the end of the Levante Beach. It was all agreed and the lads were going to book next Saturday lunchtime. After his friends had left Rob decided to get some fresh air and walk down to the shop for a can of Pepsi and some Minoltas and then spend the rest of the evening watching Match of the Day that his Mam had hopefully videoed for him as Leicester played Chelsea yesterday as it was a featured game.

It was dusk when Rob got to Mokha's Dad's shop. Sitting outside were two lads from school that he had not seen for ages, Totti and Stace. They were sat upon the 3 feet high wall outsides the shop, Totti was drinking a can of coke and Stace was drinking a pint of milk out of a Kirby and West Milk bottle.

'Oi Oi Saveloy', Stace shouted pleased to see Rob and a broad smile came upon Rob's and the lads faces, they were all genuinely pleased to see each other.

Rob sat down next to them after he had got his Pepsi and chocolate. 'How's it going Stace?' Rob asked 'Doogy Rev mate, doogy rev'. Was Stace's reply.

Rob's life seemed to follow Candide's at times and Voltaire was spot on when he wrote that life is a series of what good luck, what bad luck. However, sometimes things happen so strange in life that you can even wonder if they actually happened at all. Call it predestination, Karma or the willingness of things to happen sometimes situations arise that make one question freewill. It makes Plato's shadows re-enacting our in a cave life plausible. One of these instances was going to happen to Rob.

As the three lads caught up and talked about the old days at school a White Golf GTi Mark 1 convertible screeched to an abrupt halt immediately in front of them. Rob looked up started and straight into the eyes of the boy sitting in the passenger seat. He knew immediately who it was.

He looked into the man's eyes and the man stared at Rob. 'You facking Leicester scum', the man violently spat out in his London accent. It was the lad who Rob had punched at the Leyton Orient game years before.

Quickly Stacey replied' Meet Kirby you cunts', and with this he threw his milk pint bottle and three quarters of its white content through the car window. It hit the lad in the head and ricocheted into the windscreen inside the car spraying all its contents. Stacey followed this up by kicking the passenger door so hard with the flat of his foot that it creased the car door. The four lads in the car were stunned.

Rob ran off down Lindfield Road and Totti and Stacey ran the other way. Rob sprinted through the pathways of the old people's bungalows and he commando rolled over the wire fence and into the grounds of the convent. Did that really happen? Was it really the Chelsea lad? How the hell were they in the Leicester Western Suburbs? What should I do now? All these thoughts passed through Rob's brain as he hid in the shrubbery of the convent grounds.

Rob gave it half an hour and decided to walk home the long way up Sandringham Hill and through New Parks via the back streets to Pindar Road. Every car that passed Rob ducked into a privet hedge or garden; his nerves were heightened.

Nearly a week passed without any incident and the five lads met in Lewis's Travel shop on the first floor in the art deco monolithic leviathan of a department store. Rob tried to be the joker asking the middle-aged woman who was the travel agent but masqueraded as an air hostess in her neckerchief and American tan tights how long chicken took in her computer monitor and when she asked for 'Any Special requests?' Rob replied, 'have you anything by the Smiths?'. Both were met with an awkward smile.

They were now all booked and agreed to retire to the Pinch of Snuff for some Vodka and oranges. These were the days before all day drinking, so they had to be quick. This is where the second apparition appeared to Rob in a week. As they were walking down the spiral grand staircase in Lewis's Rob saw Ang waiting on the stairs. She had blonde hair and dark brown eyes looking like St Etienne's Sarah Cracknell and she smiled at Rob as he walked past. Once again, he wondered if this really happened or it was another ghost from his past?

Chapter 4 Summer

Sometimes things change incredibly quickly but most of the time, time ticks by. We still live in Victorian Terraced houses rather than in some super space age as predicted in the 1950's and 60's Sci-fi era. Most periods look to the past for influence, the Victorians and medieval or the Georgians and Classical times. However, the 1950's, 60's and 70's looked towards a technological scientific future where we wore lycra suits and drove jet cars. Similarly, as one century ends at midnight on December 31st and another begins a minute later January 1st the decade, century, era, period largely remains the same for years.

The summer period for Rob and his mates were however, one of those times when things changed very quickly. The boys spent more and more time together. Friday and Saturday nights were spent going out into town. A few pre club drinks in bars like Rickshaws and Winston's and then to a club on Saturdays either Legends or the Superbowl. Rob really liked guitar based indie music like New Order or the Smiths, but the clubs played mainstream R and B like Luther Vandross or Alexander O'Neill, they even had the last twenty minutes dedicated for the slow dances where punters made their last-ditch attempt of female contact. Rob often got a last dance, usually with the Casual girls in their Burberry or Aquascutum macs. Music was soon to have a massive change with the house and dance music era and DJ's being the new gods. Conversely, new guitar bands from Manchester would also be the kings of cool, The Stone Roses, Charlatans, Inspiral Carpets lay just around the corner and in the future Rob would become obsessed by these and 808 State. They were more his thing.

 A year or so later Rob was asked to go to the North West to a place called Spike Island by his friend Reuben, who had two tickets to see the Stone Roses. Reuben was as cool as a mountain stream. He was a hulk of a man, six feet tall, broad and about twenty stones in weight. He spoke slowly and considered. He dressed in his own style and he had curly blonde hair and a moon face. He was related to the Krays by his aunt's marriage. Reuben and Rob stood on some disused railway tracks at the back when The Roses came on. Reuben pulled a small tablet out of his pocket; it was pink with a picture of a bird crudely embossed into it. 'Just paid twenny five squid for this bad boy Rob, have half'. Without even thinking Rob washed it down with a swig of his can of Red Stripe. Fifteen minutes later Rob kept on feeling waves of euphoria building and swelling up insides him. Every time he fought it back. Reuben stood motionless he had emptied the content of his bowels into his denim dungarees.

Steve's behaviour became more extreme. He was a fit and strong young man of average height and he did apply to join the Parachute Regiment when he left school, but he had an awful experience at the selection centre, where the Sergeant was a bully.

The more laughs Steve got the madder his behaviour became. It began with taxi rides home on a Friday. Steve started taking a balaclava out with him and he'd pop up behind the bar in clubs and ask customers what they wanted to drink before he was forced to get to the other side of the bar. This progressed into the taxi ride home where Steve would sit in the passenger seat being normal and then turn away and put his balaclava on and say to the cabbie, 'drive!', in his gruffest deep voice.

Steve and Rob tended to get a taxi home together from the town on most Friday evenings. Rob would sit in the back and Steve in the front. Rob would be dropped off first on Pindar Road and Steve would make the mile-long journey to Braunstone Frith alone in the cab. When they reached the destination Rob would ask how much his fare was and when the driver was busy with the meter, Rob would open the door and do a runner, sprinting up the alleyways in the rabbit warren of houses. Rob just did it for the thrill and often hoped that the driver would pursue him for added excitement.

One-night Steve's plan failed. This particular night Rob was laughing to himself in the back of the taxi. When it came to his stop, he leant forward and patted Steve goodnight upon his shoulder and at the same time silently pushed the door locking knob down on his passenger front door. The taxi sped off and when it came to Steve's stop, he frantically tried to egress the taxi and couldn't work out why. Eventually to the driver's bewilderment he reached into his pocket and reluctantly paid the £5 fare.

Sundays were mostly spent with the lads going to Bradgate Park in Rob's car. Bradgate Park was a Tudor deer park and ancestral home of the Grey family. Lady Jane Grey was Queen of England for just nine days in Tudor times and the Tudor house she lived in is ruins in the middle of the landscaped country park now owned by the people of Leicestershire in trust.

When one enters through the Newtown Linford gate the park has a path that winds alongside a river on one side and has a steep hill with rocks and trees upon it. The lads would take a football and kick it along the path until the path opened up into a large grass plain where they could set up goals. Steve would pretend he was Rambo and jump down the hill into the trees shouting, 'out here I am the law'.

During the week Rob and Steve grew closer and often went for jogs and runs. Sometimes these runs would be through Bradgate, sometimes along the Grand Union Canal at Aylestone.

At work Rob worked with a girl called Kathryn, she was about five years older and Rob had been on a date with her, but the couple never had a second date. Every night Kathryn's friend Miranda would wait for her after work and occasionally make small talk with Rob. One night when Rob was pulling down the iron shutters Miranda said to him 'So Rob when are you going to take me for that drink?' Rob was taken aback drink. I've never suggested a drink. He thought and his brain took time to process her statement. He then realised that she was asking Rob out for a drink.

He looked confused and she giggled 'How about Thursday night?'

'Ok what time? And you're picking me up', she replied giggling.

'7-30? Where do you live?' Miranda replied with her address in Thurmaston. Rob had never been to that part of Leicestershire but acted like he knew it. He walked back into work pleased with himself and beaming a smile. His face was so lit up that the shop was asking questions. Rob did not tell anyone, but Kathryn knew and was secretly jealous.

Thursday came around quickly and it was a glorious sunny still evening. Rob used his Dad's 1971 Leicester A to Z with its yellowing fusty pages to find her address. Rob arrived on time and she made him knock on her front door. A silver framed Everest door with amber coloured leaf patterned glass. It was a semi-detached, private home, she was no council estate girl. Rob was intimidated by the house.

Miranda came out all smiley and cocky. She was different to other girls Rob had dated. She was chic and classy. No pound shop Kardashian. She was fashionable but not in the Chavish fashions that Rob usually dated. She was tall and elegant. Always suntanned and well made up. She moved towards Rob's car and she had a cream chino knee length skirt on with pocket detailing, white heels and a white button up blouse. She was sublimely confident and worked in an accountants in the city. By contrast Rob was a juxtaposition of having low self-esteem yet being a proud man. He was prime candidate for Cognitive Therapy.

Rob took her to the obligatory Bulls Head pub at Woodhouse Eaves and then they decided to go for a walk and talk in Bradgate Park. Rob pulled into the Old John car park which is high upon a hill with Titianesque views over Leicester, and the warm summer, golden sunshine made both the countryside and couple ooze beauty. The tarns, patchwork quilts of enclosure award fields, the clouds the summer evening sun on Cropston Reservoir looked perfect like the couple.

Young people always pick flaws with their looks or weight but in later years they realise how beautiful they really were. Even the grey monolithic Bauhaus, functionally angular grey building of Walker's Crisps in the distance was not ugly. That night. That night only.

Miranda and Rob soon became girlfriend and boyfriend, but Rob was careful just to see her a couple of nights a week as his friends were his main priority. Girlfriends ruin friendships.

<u>Chapter 5 Preparation.</u>

The weeks ticked by and the Five lads grew closer by their Friday and Saturday nights out. It is such a legacy of the industrial evolution that working-class men after a hard week at work spend their money to forget the toil of their labours in the pub.

More often than not the kebabs were replaced by an Indian meal at the end of the evening and the lads had their own Tandoori Restaurant, The Nawab on Highcross Street. It was run down and bland inside but a knock on the locked door at 1-30 AM was always opened and the lads got a basic curry and rice for a fiver. The lads always behaved which was not always the case in other establishments. It was not racism or race related. The lads behaved in high jinks after a skin full at the end of the night in any food establishment; hot dog stalls, pizza shops, chip shops and once Steve was chased down the High Street by kitchen staff from a Chinese Restaurant with cleavers!

At one up market Indian Restaurant on High Street, one Friday night, the lad's starters were interrupted by the manager. 'Who had thrown their Tandoori Chicken bones at the works party over there?' he demanded.

There was a party of about 10 well dressed in suits and shirts sitting around a round table looking over at the lads.

Boon was the only one to have had a Tandoori Chicken starter and the manager demanded where his bones were?

Boon simply said 'I've et em', The next words from the manager were 'Out, out, OUT!'

Another restaurant incident happened three weeks before B Day or Benidorm leaving day. The lads have gone out on a Saturday night to Nottingham for Kirky's birthday celebrations along with some of the Leicester Forest East and Braunstone lads. The night ended up in an underground Indian restaurant off Maid Marian Way.

There was about fifteen lads all sat along a long rectangular table that was covered by white embossed paper tablecloths. Steve sat next to Rob and opposite sat a youth called Hench. The starters and drinks were ordered. Hench was dressed in fashionable casual clothing but had long brown, permed hair which was lubricated with wet look gel. Rob could never work out if he was a handsome lad or his face was made from other people's body parts. Hench always walked, moved and spoke slowly and his voice had a kind of Californian surfer drawl and every sentence either contained the word cool or man.

Rob noticed that the waiters had lit tea light candles upon the table and without thinking he picked one up and used the flame to light the paper tablecloth. Within seconds the fire spread along the table and was burning, head high.

Surprisingly enough the lads just ignored it and carried on with their conversations as the fire raged in the subterranean eatery. The waiters appeared with fire extinguishers and sprayed the table. The fire was soon put out but most of the foam and ash hit Hench covering his white Ralph Lauren shirt. Through the mist all that could be heard was Hench 'That's not cool man! That's not cool man'.

The strangest thing then happened. The waiters brought out new tablecloths and the meal continued as if nothing had ever happened. There was a taxi minibus ordered by the restaurant for the lad's twenty-five-mile journey down the A46 and this became an ordeal for the poor driver.

In the darkness and speeding along the country dual carriage way of the A46 towards Six Hills, the hedgerows whooshed by like spectres in the night. Steve decided to lean over the front seat and over the top of the driver grabbing the steering wheel saying, 'Let me drive mate', giz a go'. The driver was petrified and shouted out in broken English 'Stop, Stop, please stop, you kill us'. He said in his Grimsby accent.

The journey then continued back into normality after the infectious laughing of the passengers. Steve was quiet and Rob thought that he was asleep. Steve was fumbling about in the darkness. The next stupid thing he did was unbelievable. He had taken his boxer shorts off and in one movement his put them over the head of the driver like a sack. It's a testament to the driver's skills and patience that the boys arrived back in postcode LE3 alive and well and they gave the driver a huge tip and vacated on good terms!

Two weeks before B Day Steve and Rob agreed to go to Nottingham and buy their holiday clothes as Leicester was limited with only Limeys, Racquet and The End Clothing stocking their styles.

They arrived in the city at Lunchtime and started their shopping spree with a pint in the Old Jerusalem Pub! Around the marketplace and arcades Rob bought a Best Company green sweatshirt [that he absolutely loved], a Radio Clothing ring spun t-shirt, a Reiss polo shirt, Joseph's Jeans and a blue Lacoste round necked jumper. They lads had a really nice day and Steve admitted to Rob that this was the first time that he'd actually owned nice clothes.

With the day being so perfect the two friends went out into town that night. Rob couldn't resist wearing his new Best Company sweatshirt. The first pub they went into as usual was Rickshaws near the Clock Tower. The pair got two pints of lager and stood talking in the half-full bar. Sometimes on Fridays if they caught the last bus home there would be trouble or an atmosphere and months before a lad called Frogging had offered Rob out and as Rob got off the bus Rob flatly kicked the seated Frogging in the face, job done. However, Frogging now entered Rickshaws and squared up to Rob. Being taught by his Dad to always get in there first, Rob nutted Frogging and caught his pint in the blow as well.

Frogging fell to the floor grabbing Rob's sweatshirt and Rob pulled away. The motion caused Robs worst fear, he hears the tare, the strain and ripping sound of his new sweatshirt. Rob was gutted. Rob did not even carry on and kick Frogging or even look to see if Frogging was going to attack. There were no bouncers around, so Rob just walked down the stairs taking his beloved new sweatshirt off on the way. He inspected the garment seeing the rip.

'I can't believe it mate', Rob said mournfully. Steve look giving his condolences. 'I am going home mate', Rob said looking down. Steve saw Dom and another painter from college and decided to stay out but he was furious his perfect day had been ruined.

Steve caught the last bus home and he was still angry. To his error up the stairs came Frogging. Steve went wild he pulled the handrail off with superhuman strength shouting at 'Frogging C'mon then!' Frogging could not believe his bad look and sprinted down the stairs and off the bus. He heard the furore as the bus trundled off down Woodgate. Steve was hitting at the bus windows being joined in the destruction by one of the older Steamer lads Zoony. The driver stopped the bus and called the Police.

Once again Voltairean predictions took control, good luck, bad luck. Steve realised that he was in trouble and sobered up. He decided the best cause of action was to open the upstairs back window of the double decker bus and escape. Steve opened the window and dangled himself down by his hands so to lower the drop.

'Thud', the fall stung Steve's feet and he dropped to his knee briefly. He ran through the factories and old dye mills as running along the main roads he would easily be picked up by the Police. He climbed onto a factory roof and saw a grey concrete yard below that he lowered himself down the wall onto.

'Splash', the cold waist deep water and shock took Steve's breath away. He was confused. The grey yard was not a yard at all but the River Soar. He was now stuck in the margins plodgin with no way out as steep factory walls were the banks. It was silent except for the shrill of a scared coot, which made Steve constantly jump. He thought that the only way out was to make his way towards a bridge, so he struggled through the margins to Frog Island. Luck had it that there were two men stood talking après pub upon the bridge.

One said to the other 'Hey Mick there's someone down there in the river'. They both strained their eyes in the dark and saw the zombie figure of Steve, struggling along.

'You alright mi duck?' one of the men shouted down and now Steve was closer returned 'Can you pull me up if I climb up this drain pipe a bit please?' Steve climbed up the drainpipe as far as he could, and it broke with the rust and his hands and fingers dented it and poked holes through it.

He held out a hand and one of the men grasped it, leaning over the bridge railing and pulled. He struggled and his larger companion grasped Steve's other hand and they managed to drag his sodden body over the rail and to safety on the pavement. Steve explained how he'd been beaten up and thrown into the river and they men bought the story and wanted to call the Police.

Steve quickly declined their offer and profusions thanked them before making his own way home along Groby Road.

Steve was still wet and bedraggled when he got home. His Dad was still up. His Dad looked up from Prisoner Cell Block

H and said 'Bloody Hell what's happened to ye like?' Steve used the same answer he had before about being attacked and thrown into the canal.

'Reet, I'm calling the Pole leece'. Was his father's reply. Steve protested that it was his own fault and begged his Dad not to call the Police.

His Dad smelling there was a rabbit off relented and it was too late to argue with his son so left it with one last sentence. 'I divvunt think it's right like, take that wet clobber off it's covered in clarts and all sorts and ha'way to bed son. Bloody hoyed into the canal, I bet it's that Derek's fault'. With that Steve took his sodden clothes off, put them on top of the twin tub and went to bed.

Chapter 6 Alternate Universes

As B Day was now only a week away, there were already Leicester lads away on their holidays. Lads that Rob either knew already or un beknown to him would enter his life at a later date, like DNA codes being released throughout our lives.

Cog was a butcher, younger than Rob by a year or two and his Mother had taught Rob Religious Education at school, years before. He was a good looking, thin lad with nice permed hair and a sharp Weller-like face. He had confidence and always pulled girls, telling them that he was a hairdresser. His mate was Kris. He was the same age as Cog, once again full of swagger like a young Liam Gallagher.

They were already on holiday in Falaraki in Rhodes and had been there a week. Both suntanned golden brown and had at least two girls each back to their apartment. On one-night Cog had pulled a young lass from Blackpool. He took her back and had sex with her in the double bed that he shared with Kris. When Kris got back and got into the bed there was Cog, the lass and Kris like sardines in the bed. Kris felt a wet, sticky fluid on the sheets near his thigh.

' What the Fuck's this Cog'?

'Oh, I had to lubricate her with your hair gel mate', was the reply.

In the night the naked girl climbed over Kris and had a piss in the sink next to Kris's head. She then picked up Kris's shirt and dried her vagina with it in a forward to back motion.

'Did you see that fucker Cog? 'Kris asked.

'Yeah bloody amazing'.

On the eighth night a boy of about 25 years who was working in Faliraki selling drinks from a cool box on the beach was in the Jet night club. Every day he walked the hot beach with his cool box shouting in his thick scouse accent, 'Coke, Fanta, Sprite and all that shite'.

The tall balding, ginger Scouser bumped into Kris's back at the bar when he was being lairey. Kris turned around to see what had happened and the guy just looked at Kris scornfully and said 'Fuck off Shaggy 'and carried on showing off to some giggling girls.

Kris tapped him on the shoulder' What did you fucking say son?' The scouser turned around and squared up to Kris. 'Fuck off now and do one, before you get one.' With that Kris said, 'oh alright mate', and pulled out his disposable Stanley knife and cut the Scouser across the cheek in a slashing motion.

The girls screamed and the Scouser held his cheek. Bouncers and Police apprehended Kris and took him to the Police cells. Kris was put in a large cell that had iron bars on three sides and reminded him of a cell in a Western Cowboy film. During the course of the night, more and more tourist was put into this cell with their cuts and ripped and bloody clothes.

Kris was starting to get a hangover; it was hot, and he was dehydrated. A lad sitting on a wooden bench across the cell with his head in his hands had a bottle of water. Kris walked over to him and said, 'Can I have a drink of your water mate please?'

The man looked up 'Fuck off, you slashed my face a couple of hours ago!' Kris was deported the next day on a flight to London rather than East Midland's, just to be difficult for him.

Another alternate holiday that was happening at the same time was with the Anstey lads. The five men on this holiday all played rugby together and drank hard. On the day that they had to fly out to Magaluf they met at noon in the Coach and Horses Pub. After a two-hour, power hour they got in the minibus taxi to the airport. Big fat Mick was already asleep by the time they had left the Village. Butler [already 32 on this 18-30 holiday] ripped up a cigarette packet and placed it between Mick's toes as he had flip flops and shorts on. Stroudy lit eat bit of cardboard and Mick snored away. The smell of burning flesh was horrible and Mick woke up shouting in pain and holding his burning left foot, he was in agony.

As their holiday wore on Mick's foot got infected from dirty streets, nightclubs and sand. It got bigger and bigger and he had to cut the toe section out of his left trainer. To add insult to injury the rugby boys decided to go out in fancy dress one night. Mick was going to go as a green devil, goblin type character. However, un beknown to him. Howard had got him some green body paint but as Howard was a printer, he had mixed it with green dye. Similarly, because Stroudy was a carpet fitter he had smeared super strength carpet glue onto micks' horns that went on his bald head.

The night was a great laugh with Rasper as Arnold Schwarzenegger dressed as commando, but the real laugh came the next day. Big Mick was in the shower and couldn't get either the green ink off him or the horns off. He was cursing, slamming about and he burst out of the bathroom door like the hulk, naked. He was going ballistic trying to swing at the lads who through fits of laughter ducked Mick's blows until he slipped on the wet floor onto his bad food and howled with pain.

After he had calmed down Butler and Stroudy pulled at his horns, but they would not budge. So, Butler cut them off just leaving the plastic stumps attached. Poor Mick spent the next ten days of his holiday limping around, dyed green with two horn stumps on his head like a green Hell Boy. Bizarrely enough Mick was propositioned by more than one gay man that week.

Ten years later Rob was to go on tour with the Anstey lads as he started to play rugby for them. It was an Easter tour to Hamburg playing against the British Army at Bergen-Belsen.

After the long min bus journey Rob had to share a room with Stroudy and Young Bryn. The room was nicknamed the Room of Mong. Bryn's younger brother had once played on the wing for Anstey and the opponents once shouted 'Kick it to the mong on the wing'. Stroudy was the team captain, a tall, talented, bald man who was excellent at giving and taking insults.

The first night out was in a nightclub in the village of Bergan. The strangest thing was that every time anyone danced the bouncers would appear and stop it shouting' No danzing!'. Apparently, because it was Good Friday! All the lads were suitably drunk and headed back to the barracks in dribs and drabs.

Rob was sharing a taxi with Rasper. When arriving at the security point, the soldier approached the car and Rob wound the window down. 'Can you identify yourselves gents please?' was the soldier's question.

Rob turned the rear-view mirror towards his face and replied 'yep it's me'. Non plussed the soldier got Rob and Rasper out of the car. After a dressing down by him on the needs of security the two had to walk the mile to the barracks through the camp. Two mad things happened that night.

Rob got into bed and he was the only one in the Room of Mong. He had just entered REM sleep when he heard the incessant knocking on the door. Rob reluctantly got out of bed and let Stroudy in who walked straight past Rob like a Zombie and straight into the bathroom. Rob went back to bed. He didn't know if he'd been asleep for an hour or five minutes, but he could see the light in the bathroom and the sound of the shower.

Rob thought that he'd better have a look and got out of bed again and entered the bathroom. Through the frosted glass of the shower pod he could see the outline of Stroudy. He opened the shower cabinet door and there he was, soaking wet in his blazer, shirt, trousers and water filled shoes. The shower was running full blast making a noise like an angry storm.

Stroudy turned and looked blankly at Rob and said, 'Thank God you've come Rich, I've been banging on this door for over an hour and it's not stopped chucking down of rain'. And with that Stroudy walked past Rob took his clothes off and got into his bed! His clothes were in a soggy pile on the floor.

Rob wondered where Young Bryn was? He was soon to find out. He heard an earth shuddering 'Agghhhhhhgrr', from outside the room. Rob shot out of bed and opened the door. There was Young Bryn standing Like a scarecrow and hyperventilating. One by one the tourist's doors opened. Bryn had fallen asleep, drunken in the corridor. Rasper and Gilbert had found him and had a dump on his neck. They had then taken Bryn's wallet out and took his debit card and smeared the brown excrement over his nose, mouth and face.

Matters got worse for Bryn as the tour continued. Rob used his suitcase as a portable commode on the last day and wiped his bottom on his white shirt leaving a large brown tyre track across it and closing it back up so it would spend the journey back to the U.K with its little surprise waiting to greet Bryn upon his return. The final straw was Butler gluing Mr pringle faces that he had cut out from a tube of Pringles over Young Bryn's passport photograph.

Chapter 7 B-Day

The flight was a night flight from East Midlands Airport to Alicante on Sunday. On Saturday Rob decided to take Miranda out for a meal and have an early night. He picked her up in his Mark 2 Escort and he had booked a table at the Cottage in the Wood Restaurant in Woodhouse Eaves.

It was the first real time that Rob had been to a restaurant. He was slightly intimidated. They were shown to a table and given menus. Rob remembered his French lessons [God bless Miss Thompson] and ordered a bottle of Muscadet wine with the correct pronunciation. On the menu there was a fruit juice starter. This confused Rob. A glass of orange or grapefruit juice as a starter! He ordered a prawn cocktail. For his main course he ordered Rainbow

Trout and it stared back at him from the plate. He just picked at the fish. A bad choice.

After the meal Rob took Miranda home and said that he would call her tomorrow afternoon. She asked if she could pop around and see his Mam and Dad when he was away. Rob was taken aback 'Of course you can, but why?'

'For tea', she giggled 'I like them, they're cute'. She really wanted to keep in touch and stake her claim for Rob whilst he was away. Their parting kiss was lingering, and Miranda held Rob's face. 'Don't kiss any Spanish girls.

The red Escort pulled onto the drive. 'You're back early Son', Rob's Dad said, he was watching the Likely Lads' film.

Rob grabbed a can of Coke out of the fridge and sat on the settee. The melancholic yet funny storyline appealed to Rob. How Bob was jealous of Terry's single life and how there was unrequited chemistry between Velma and Terry. Rob and his Dad laughed out loud to Terry playing God's voice as Bob crossed Wallsend High Street.

After the film had finished Rob's Dad went to the back door to smoke another salt peter Park Drive and Rob changed channels on the Television and a Steptoe and Son film was on BBC2. Rob became engaged with the film as Harold Steptoe got married and went on honeymoon to Spain, with his Dad. Eventually Rob was tired enough to overcome the excitement of the forthcoming day.

Sunday morning started like any other. Rob's Mam and Nan made bacon and tomatoes on toast. Rob brought his suitcase down from upstairs and wrote out and attached the paper Thompson luggage label to the plastic handle. The case was green and made from a material that Rob did not recognise. It was the same case that had been used on the couple of family holidays that he'd been on with his Mam and Nan to Butlin's in Skegness or Southsea. It was a funny in-between age even Rob's suitcase had links to his childhood but was filled with clothes for adulthood.

The day passed slowly, and Rob called Miranda at 2-30 as promised. 'what you up to tonight?'

'Just going out with Kate, quiet drink and catch up, her blokes such a dick. Just going to the Golf Range or Meridian'.

'I'll bell you a couple of times when I'm away and send you a card'.

'You'd better', was the response and after the formality of the goodbyes she was gone. Rob was to find out months later that, in the evening Miranda was going out with her Friend Kate and two guys to the Durham Ox Nightclub.

Rob was being picked up by Boon's Dad at 6 PM. The other lads were being taken to the airport by Dayle's Dad in his old Volvo estate car as they all lived in the Braunstone Frith area.

At 6 on the dot the new Ford Capri Laser pulled up outside Rob's house. Both Boon and his Dad got out of the car to greet Rob who had left the house. Boon shook hands and opened the hatchback for the green suitcase. The two parents stood talking and Rob's Dad insisted upon giving Boon's Dad petrol money. Rob sat in the back of the white Capri and he thought that it was the most aesthetically pleasing car that he'd ever seen. He likened it to sitting in Concorde sitting in the back in the styled separate seats. The dash looked like a cockpit and the cramped interior, whist uncomfortable it was exciting and stylish and when on the M1 Motorway it felt like the car was doing 170 miles an hour not 70. When they pulled into the drop off zone the rest of the group were already unloading their cases from the Volvo's boot.

Before the group even spoke, Dez just stood there pointing at Dayle's Suitcase. It was huge and was made of carpet material with a 70's flock to it, like a cheap Indian Restaurant. Rob asked, 'good to see we are all here ok'.

Dez replied 'Yep no probs' with traffic, especially Dayle who got here on his magic carpet'. He was still laughing and pointing at the suitcase. The lads entered the airport and seen on the monitors that their Britannia Airway's flight to Alicante was check in Desk 12. At check Rob asked for extra leg room.

'Do you have a back or leg problem sir?' The Customer Service Agent asked.

'Yes, I've got Athletes' Foot'.

After check in and finding out they were all on one row at the rear of the aircraft they headed off for food after waving goodbye to their suitcases and the flying carpet.

The Croc Pot was the name of the airport restaurant and it had a life size figure of a green crocodile holing a cauldron at its entrance. Rob said that it looked like Dayle and said, 'Let's have a photo of you and ya twin mate'.

Dayle dutifully stood next to the hard-plastic statue and Rob used his new Swatch camera to take the picture. The camera was rubbish and Rob had to press very hard to get the shutter button down and it hurt his thumb to wind the film on with the little plastic grooved wheel. Rob knew the photo would be blurred.

The lads had all made the effort to wear decent clothes for the flight. Rob was in double denim. Jeans and a denim jacket with cord collars, light blue Adidas Gazelle trainers and a royal blue Lacoste polo shirt. Steve was also in double denim with leather collars with a blue and white Benneton rugby shirt beneath. All the lads ordered the all-day breakfast and Dayle added 'Just in case all we get to eat is that Dago foreign rubbish'. Boon was the odd one out and ordered a pizza. When it arrived, it was like the World's first English attempt at making a pizza. It was literally a loaf of bread with melted cheese and sliced tomatoes on the top. Boon was disgusted and punched it!

The next stop was the bar and as they reached the top of the stairs there were people everywhere. Groups of lads, groups of girls. Sitting on the floor, sitting on stools or standing in groups. It seemed like the whole of humanity in the East Midlands was going away on holiday. The group got their lagers and stood near the windows looking upon the runway. Rob saw a rogue flash of lightning behind the darkening silhouettes of the cooling towers in the distance. Halfway through their pints, their flight was called and after many queues and Dayle being stopped in security for having a huge pair of scissors for 'cutting his toe nails' in his hand luggage they boarded the aircraft by the rear doors and took their seats on the back row.

In front of them sat some older lads. They were well lubricated and loud. Rob felt like a little boy and intimidated by their loud and brashness. He hated their Burtons and Top Man clothes, their mullet hair, moustaches and their Nottingham accents. 'Divs', he thought.

As the plane was pushed back, the air hostesses began their safety routine. The blokes in front heckled.

'Hey air hostess. You can cut my hair anytime darling. Hey darling forget the life jacket toggle you can come here and pull my toggle hard'.

Rob looked at Boon, he was looking for something to throw at the men. The mood passed as the distraction of the take-off took hold and after levelling off the food and drinks service began. Rob had been waiting to buy some decent aftershave and bought a Lacoste men's fragrance that came in a white bottle that looked like a little polo shirt. Steve bought some Kourous and the strong smell helped douse the smell of cigarettes and smoke from the smoking rear end of the plane.

The flight was uneventful and so was customs and a stern Thompson representative, a lady in her late thirties, not happy about greeting drunken working-class people on a night flight, met the with her clipboard 'Lead passenger's name! Coach stand 3'. She had an unapproachable, direct manner and would have done well in the German SS.

The first thing that the lads noticed was the heat, even at night. Their bags were loaded under the coach and they were off into the Iberian night. Silhouettes of huge bulls with huge cojones stood on the hillsides, made of wood. They drove through small towns which reminded Rob of Spaghetti westerns and he kept on repeating the phrases 'Hey Gringo, Hey Blondie'.

It's always worse arriving in a different country at night and the apprehension rose as people began to get dropped off in nice hotels, lit up receptions with porters and staff. The lads were soon the last ones on the bus. The coach crawled up a hill at the very end of the Levante Beach and into a dark car park. No staff, no reception. The rep got off the bus and returned from a dark entrance hall with a sealed envelope with the name Robert Sutton on the front, apartment 192.

'Some welcome this lads', Boon said sarcastically. The bags were unloaded, and the group entered the marble entrance hall, where a light came on automatically. The stainless-steel doors opened, and they packed into the elevator to the nineteenth floor. Rob unlocked the door and they entered the large apartment. It was very nice, nicer than any of the lad's houses. Rooms were chosen. Rob and Dayle in one room, Boon on his own and Steve and Dez in the other. They were so excited, running around the room hooting and hollering opening cupboards and draws.

Boon found a football in a cupboard left behind by a previous tenant. He began doing keepie-uppies until Steve got hold of the ball and volleyed it out of his hands and in a double whammy broke the lampshade and the ball thudded from the electric junction box fusing all the apartment lights but one, which was in the main living area and the bathroom light. Rob ventured outside onto the balcony and Benidorm looked twinkling and beautiful as the lights spread around the large sweeping crescent of sand.

Rob looked down and an angry man below looked up and said in his Manc' accent. 'Is it you making that fucking noise?'

Rob replied, 'What fucking noise you Northern Monkey?' and with that the retort was higher pitched and angry. 'What noise! What noise? I'll show you what fucking noise!'

Thud! Thud! Thud! 'Don't answer the door Dayle, it's that geezer from downstairs', Rob said. Too late Dayle opened the door, and the man burst in. he grabbed Dayle around the throat and pinned him to the wall in one movement.

'Any more noise and I'll kill all of ya! It's 3-45 in the morning' no one spoke and thank heavens; Boon was on the toilet.' Get it? Get it?' the man shouted, and the boys nodded feeling childish. Then he was gone.

Chapter 8 B-Day plus one

A new day dawned, and Rob walked onto the balcony. They were so high up when he spat over the balcony, he couldn't see his spittle reach anywhere near the floor. The front balcony looked out over Levante Beach whilst the back looked upon some scrubland and a rocky bay.

Buenos Aries, Rob wondered where he had heard the name before. He cast his mind back to his childhood and remembered. It was the 1978 Argentinian World Cup. It was one of the hosting cities.

Rob remembered his Panini stickers and the blue collector's book that he filled. He remembered playing football on the green whilst the older Steven Mitchell commentated, and rein acted Cubillas's goal for Peru and Archie Gemmill's wonder goal for Scotland against Holland.

considering that it was such a late night. Slowly by slowly the lads appeared on the balcony relatively early. The conversation was all about the angry man from last night. 'I wonder how ya mate is this morning Dayle?' Dez said and he sniggered loudly like Muttley.

Dayle threw the birdy finger back. The sea glistened in the sunshine and it sparked a lovely deep blue. Steve looked out. He lost his breath at the beauty. His eyes scanned the island in the bay, the inviting sea, the golden arc of sand and the high rise behind it. He struggled to process and comprehend the scene. He'd never seen such beauty; he'd never been on holiday before.

The group decided an English breakfast and buying pop for the room was first on the agenda. They piled into the steel lift to the ground floor. Dez rocked the lift and Dayle's eyes grew wide with fear. The egressed from the apartment block to the front where there was a large rectangular pool, with no one around or in it. A further elevator took the lads to street level. As they walked through the winding back street, a smell Rob had never smelt before filled his nostrils. It was the acrid smell of warm sewage from the sewers. 'Pwhoar gawd

blimey Dayle is that your aftershave?'
Rob said screwing his face up.

'Wild Stallion, smells of horses', Steve
joined in. 'He makes it from dead cats,
like that one there', said Dez pointing at
a grey, decomposing, roadkill, cat in the
gutter. 'Pulls all the pussy', was Dayle's
pervy response. At the bend in the road
was a Spanish owned café, a Spanish
greasy spoon. The boys sat at 2 tables
covered with vinyl tablecloths and Rob's
forearms sweated onto the sticky table.
After their overcooked bacon and
sausage, tinned mushrooms and fried
eggs swimming with little pools of olive
oil, the lads went next door to the shop,
and each bought a 2-litre bottle of pop.
As a boy Rob's Mam would buy him 3
bottles of pop from the Alpine man. He

used to hate it if they got the order wrong and gave him the hideous cream soda or Dandelion and Burdock.

After walking back to the apartment to drop the drinks off. They got changed ready for the beach. Back on the road Boon had yellow Spurs shorts on, Rob similarly wore football shorts but white Umbro Leicester City. Dez and Steve wore Adidas running shorts which were made of nylon and were very short. Dayle wore a Hawaiian Shirt and budgie smugglers with espadrilles on his feet.

They settled in the corner of the beach and laid their towels down. Rob took his shorts off to reveal his old school burgundy speedos, but the s had fallen off the front of the label! Steve ran straight into the warm Mediterranean

Sea, diving like Tarzan. He absolutely could not describe how he felt in this new world.

Rob lay besides Dayle and as the day wore on, he saw the colour of Dayle's flesh change colour. Rob could not tell what colour from behind his black Rayban Wayfarer copies. 'You'd better put some suntan lotion on mate'. With that Dayle withdrew a bottle of factor 2 oil. 'Dayle you're blonde, son. You're gonna fry in that bad boy'.

'Ahhhh'. Dayle dismissed Rob and rubbed it in. 'Aghhhhhhh', was Dayle's next words 'My eyes, my f eyes!' Rob looked at him. Dayle's eyes were bulging and red. He'd got lotion into them. Dayle was up and dancing holding his face. The beach was red hot under his feet, burning his soles so he also screamed and hoped with that. It looked like Dayle was doing an African Cultural dance. Dez was in hysterics.

Dez wanted to live his life. He embraced new challenges and was game for anything. In the future he would attempt to climb Mount Everest, but the cable ski was his Everest today. In the corner of Levante Beach there was a contraption that ran on cables suspended 20 feet above the sea level. From these cables ran a rope that went around the rectangles of cables for about 500 metres out to sea and back again. To get on this ride one must wade out to a platform, pay your money, clamp your water skis on and crouch and wait for the rope to come around and hey presto, one is towed along water skiing.

Dez was dying for a go and asked Rob and Steve to go with him to hold his camera and wallet. The boys waded out 50 metres to the platform and climbed upon the wooden jetty. Dez handed his money over and he was instructed how to crouch and ski. He was given a red life jacket and the straps were pulled tight.

His turn soon came around and Dez was crouching in his skis. The cable rope came around. Dez was concentrating, his breath in quick gasps. One last grasp and groan and he grabbed the rope and was connected to the cable. Just as it began to lift him off the platform and onto the water Rob stepped on the back of Dez's skis. The power of the motor pulled Dez clean out of his bindings and dragged him along in the water dangling like a rag doll. The instructor shouted 'Let go! Let go!' Dez being stubborn would not let go and the machine dragged his flopping body out to sea.

Rob and Steve were hurting from laughing. Their sides were like someone had stuck daggers between their ribs. They couldn't breathe. Steve had even managed to take some photographs of Dez being ripped from the skis and into the water. Dez eventually had to let go and the instructor picked him up in a boat and brought him back.

'Looked good from here Dez'. Rob said. 'You're an absolute twat Rob, do ya know that? Dez replied.

'I knew you'd blame me Dez, I bet you think losing your trainers at the Pistols gig was me too?'

'It fucking was you'. Rob was laughing his head off and through his laughing said, 'It wasn't'.

Earlier in the year Dez and Rob had gone to see the Sex Pistols in Hyde Park. They were at the front and it was rammed. Dez was pogoing and as he jumped up the guy behind him stood on his heels and Dez was pulled clean out of his Adidas Forest Hills trainers blamed Rob and his trainers were never to be seen again. Dez managed to find some old sandals in the park and endure Rob singing' Too cold to touch, too hot to handle, here comes Dez in his 3-buckle sandal,' for the whole National Express journey home.

The odd thing about sunburn is that it's never apparent when it's happening, it's often not until you get indoors that the extent is discovered. This was not the case for pale Dayle. Upon their return Dayle was luminous.

'Kin hell Dayle, you need to get out of the currant bun mate, I can feel the heat from you from here', Dez said. Rob felt responsible for Dayle as he was the youngest and said, 'C'mon mate, let's go back, chill, get some grub and then get ready to go out'. With that statement the gang picked up their towels and headed back to the apartment.

Back in the apartment the lads went for a nanna nap. Rob looked at the red

Dayle on the white sheets and went to the fridge and got his after-sun lotion out for him.

'Have a go on this pal'. Dayle whimpered and inhaled deeply as he put the bright white lotion onto his legs and torso. Then 'Aggghhhh' my eyes'.

'You stupid plonker. How can you get that into your mince pies, again, you idiot?'

After their nana nap the group decided to go out for food. Boon remembered this place that he went to when he was young in The Square called The Wishing Well. The café/bar was English owned and little more than a room with a terrace that was hemmed in by two plastic walls.

Marked for Death starring Steven Segal was on the many television sets. The tables were vinyl tablecloth covered like the café earlier. There were laminated menu cards sat upright in plastic holders and the yellow cards were dog eared. Behind the bar the couple that ran it with their daughter all looked miserable and the wife came over to take the lad's orders.

'What yous having?' she said in Yorkshire accent, without smiling. The lads all ordered Cokes except for Dayle the lobster who ordered a pint of San Miguel. 'Pints or halves of Cokes boys?' was her reply. Rob had never had a pint of Coke before and when it arrived it was in a pint jug. The food was ordered egg, beans and chips all round. It was cheap and a large portion but the

Wishing Well staff argued with each other, the food was almost as sour as them.

The lads headed back to the apartment except for Steve who was making a deposit in the bar's toilet and Rob who said that he's wait for him. Steve appeared ten minutes later 'Just dropped kids off at the pool mate', he said pleased with himself. Rob just shook his head.

As the pair walked through the square, two girls around the age of twenty sat on a bar wall in the early evening sun. They both wore short denim skirts and white vest tops. 'Beachcomber tonight lads?' one asked in a Scouse accent. Rob looked up and saw that the bar was called Beachcomber. He was taken aback that they were so forward.

'What's it like?' Steve asked. 'It's boss you two will love it'.

'Will you two be there then?' Robs asked. 'Of course, we will, we love it'. The girls giggled.

'See you later then mi duck', Rob said, and the pair walked on. The lads were so naïve they did not realise that the girls were reps. 'Can't believe it Bruv, here less than 24 hours and we've pulled', Steve said.

'Unreal'.

On the road back to the apartment two lads approached Rob and Steve with a bottle in their hands. Rob said to Steve, 'here we go mate'. The lads were steaming drunk and Scottish, they stopped to speak. 'Who do ye support boys?' was the blonde-haired lad's question. Unbeknown to Rob and Steve this was a sectarian question were they Celtic or rangers, Hibs or Hearts, Catholic or protestant?

Rob thought odd question but said 'Leicester City mate'. The Scots lads smiled.

'Ah ya belter. Jock Fucking Wallace, ha some o' this Dubious, aint ne Bucky but it'll fuck ye, I'm Billy with the ten-foot willy and this is Jai'. Rob declined but the bottle was forced into his hand. Rob took a swig of the lukewarm fortified wine that said Dubois on the label and gave it to Steve for a swig.' Come on tae fuck boys get it in ye'.

'Where ye staying boys?' Was the next question. 'In the Brunos Haries Apartments', Steve replied. 'Us too', the bald one replied. Where ya gannin the noo?'

Back to get ready to go out, how about you?' In unison the Scots said, 'For a chicken supper'. They both laughed and sang a rhyme 'Can ye gan a chicken supper Bobby Sands, Can ye gan a chicken supper Bobby sands? Can you gan a chicken supper, ya dirty Fenian Fucker? Can you go a chicken supper Bobby sands'? With that sectarian lyrically they staggered off arms around shoulders down the street.

When Steve and Rob got into the lift there was a naked Scottish lad also with a bottle of fortified wine. He was standing up asleep and drunken. Every time he leant back, he got a static electric shock on his arse and it stirred him awake for a second, then back to sleep. Heaven knows how long he'd been in the lift.

Chapter 9 Benidorm Nights

The lads were quite naïve also when it came to what time to go out or what to wear. They thought that they had better go out at 8PM as they did at home.

The golden late evening sunshine made the landscape, seascape and townscape glow. This Mediterranean light was filled with beauty and anticipation and the sound of thousands of hairdryers and cassette recorders were the soundtrack to the town. Their own cassette player boomed out U2's album The Joshua Tree, and With or Without You. It was Dez's choice. Steve struggled through the living area with his mattress.

'What you are doing dog boy?' Boon asked. 'Too hot, in there with Disco Dez last night so I'm sleeping on the balcony from now on'. With that he flopped his mattress down. All the group were now ready for their first night out Rob wore clothes that he's wears in Leicester; Timberland boat shoes, Farah hopsack trousers, Lacoste polo shirt and a Sergio

Tacchini white and blue V-necked jumped. Not exactly Mediterranean wear.

The real treat was Dayle's outfit. Dayle had got a loan for his holiday clothes. He emerged from the toilet in a white linen suit. His sunburn scorched out beneath it! To complement the look, he had a white and red Hawaiian shirt and espadrille white shoes! 'Oh my God, Christ on a bike, it's Club Tropicana'. Dez said and he got the customary birdie reply.

The lads walked along the Promenade past families promenading in the late evening summer sun. They decided to head to The Square and the first bar they passed up a side street they were accosted by a girl in the obligatory denim skirt and vest top, who asked them to go in with vouchers for free shots. It was called the Silver Dollar Bar. The lads did not need much persuading. The bar was not much more than a tunnel. Some plastic tables on the street tunnelled by two plastic screens and a small room and bar at the bottom. A group of Asian lads sat on one side. Steve nudged Boon and whispered out of the side of his mouth, 'The Wongs'. The Asian lads all sat, Stoney faced not talking or smiling like a gang from the film The warriors.

The lads entered the room and the music playing was Whitney Houston's I want to Dance with Somebody'. [A few months earlier Steve had gone to the North east to visit family in Cramlington, a soulless new town in South West

Northumberland full of roundabouts, hedges, link roads and fences. No sign of human life lived there. Just rumours of people inhabiting the areas behind cheap B and Q creosoted fences. His family had taken him to thee Northern Social Club in Ashington and the turn that was on was a cover of Whitney Houston called Whitley Bay Houston!]

As the lads approached the bar in the Silver Dollar, the DJ's voice came over the mike. 'Here they are, Thomas Magnum with his do it yourself perm, his mate dressed for winter and Alf Garnett on the end'. The DJ had such a cheeky smile and laughing eyes that the lads couldn't be angry with him and warmed to him immediately. Dez laughed and sniggered because he had not mentioned him or Steve. The man behind the tiny bar was of middle age and Spanish and immediately warmed to and liked by the gang. His name was Pedro and he shook hands and gave a formal introduction.

The DJ was entertaining, he was constantly promoting his Silver Dollar, do me a favour fuck off, t-shirts which were on sale behind the tiny bar, only in white and either t-shirt or oversized vest. The DJ spoke over records and was scathing to people outside and punters and every now and again he would say his rap. 'I'm Barnsley Bill and I'm the best, I can do it in my undies, I can do it in my vest. I can do it in the morning and do it in the night, do it on the toilet whilst I'm having a shite'.

The lads stayed in the bar having some craic with Pedro and the DJ and drinking their 2 for 1 happy hour lagers. They were all pissed when they decided to move on up the street to Lennon's Bar. Steve hit the dancefloor moving ungainly and gyrating his snake hips to' Electrica Salsa, do dah dudah, doo be do da dah, dooby do dah'.

More 2 for 1 pint in the beachcomber and more still in Jimmy's Bar. The lads turned the corner and were lost. 'I know a shortcut', Steve said, and the lads followed him climbing over walls and fences until they dropped down into a lawned, walled area with music playing and a small pool. There were trellis tables with food and wine on. It was a private party in a private villa. There were so many people there that the lads just mingled in. It was a villa hired by some friends from the Derbyshire Police force and all would have been fine if Steve had not tried to headbutt his way out of the bathroom door. He was ejected out of the party but climbed back in over the wall.

Caught again by a Policewoman, she said 'I thought we'd thrown you out'? Steve Replied touching his nose with his forefinger 'CID mate'.

It was time to leave and Rob went to get some food, and everyone had got split up. Back at the apartment Dayle was hurting and whimpering in the darkness in bed, Dez was drunk and kept on putting his hands in a sink of water and then placing them on the broken electricity junction box. Sparks would fly across the dark room and Dez would shout 'I've got the power'. The sparks lit up the room like fireworks or welding. Dez was either becoming Frankenstein's Monster or super charging himself into a superhero.

Dez then decided to tightrope walk across the balcony 200 feet in the air, He fell off and Dayle panicked thinking that Dez had fallen to his death only to see Dez snoring fast asleep on the balcony. Rob managed to stumble into a takeaway and order a burger with a fried egg on top. He waddled home, one step forward, one step back whilst eating the rancid burger. When he entered the apartment, the room was dark and quiet. He got undressed and flopped onto his bed. The room started spinning. Rob hated this because when it stopped, he knew he'd be sick. It stopped and he knew he couldn't make the toilet and rushed to the balcony. He didn't make it over the balcony ledge and spewed over the balcony floor.

Drunken sleeps are always restless, and Rob awoke early with the horrors. He remembered being sick and then thought. Steve sleeps on the balcony! He ventured outside and saw that the early morning sun had dried the brown sick into refried beans.

He looked at Steve, who had brown spew all over his face and head. Thinking quickly Rob shook Steve awake. 'Steve, Steve, you've been sick in your sleep, you could have died mate'.

Steve opened one eye 'It was you, I watched ya'. What sort of bloke lies in another's sick? Rob went back to bed after taking a swig out of everyone's pop in the fridge.

In the first week, the days were spent recovering from the nights either by the pool or in bed. One afternoon Rob and Steve went out for a walk and found a shop that sold weapons. Steve bought a cosh and a canister of C.S Gas and Rob bought a smoke bomb. Back in the apartment Dez was asleep in bed so the pair thought it would be a great laugh to set the smoke bomb off in his room. Rob found a box of matches in the kitchen drawer and set about trying to light the solid chemical block at the bottom of Dez's bed. It was near impossible to light then Dez awoke. 'What the f? You're trying to set fire to my bed'.

'Don't be ridiculous', Rob replied, and the two lads decided to join Boon by the pool. 'What you two nutters doing down here? I'm surprised you two dares show your faces after throwing all the plates off the balcony like frisbees last night'. Rob and Steve had no recollection. They all lay bad on the plastic sun loungers looking up at the apartment block.

'What the hell's that?' Boon said. They all looked up and plumes of white smoke flowed from their apartment. 'the smoke bomb must have worked!' Steve said. It looked like the Towering Inferno or a terrorist attack, the pair were worried initially as it would have been seen all over Benidorm. However, no alarms sounded, and no sirens came. The smoke cleared as quickly as it had appeared. Dez never even woke up. When the lads returned to the apartment Dez appeared. 'Who's been cooking bacon?'

Chapter 10 Vicky

The lads discovered Top of The Pops Bar and nightclub. It was underground, vibrant, rammed full and sweaty. The lads got 2 for 1 drinks and Rob was on the Brandy and Coke. Push by Salt and Pepper came on and the lads hit the crowded dancefloor. 'This song is only for the sexy people'.

Dez turned to Dayle 'You'd better fuck off now then mate'. He gave his usual Muttley laugh.

Soon after the dancefloor was cleared and cordoned off. Dry ice was released like a primordial fog. A glass and stainless steel, silver machine was pushed into the centre of the dancefloor. It had 4 or 5 rotating and pumping 10-inch rubber dildos protruding out of it. Rob said to Dez 'What the Fuck?'.

Then Sticky Vicky was announced by the DJ. This naked, blonde, emaciated woman appeared and after conducting contortionist acrobatics on the machine, she continued to pull flags out of her foof and undo the crowd's beer bottle tops with her fanny. She opened Dayle's Beer and he licked the bottle top before putting the whole top end into his gob. Rob's face was one of disgust.

Rob and Steve had seen similar things before but not as extreme. They had been to the topless barmaids' night at The Flying Horse in Markfield but only stopped for one beer. Steve the old bint behind the bar with the droopy tits and stockings poured beer that was lukewarm, and you could put a flake in it.

Similarly, they had gone to a Gentlemen's evening in a pub in Market Bosworth with the Red Cow Lads. Three strippers did a turn in front of a behind locked doors crowd. Then a pint pot came around for a whip round and the three raspberry rippers picked 3 blokes from the crowd to shag on stage. Rob was uneasy, the place was full of lower working-class thugs and he thought that it might kick off anytime. Rumour has it that a West Indian lad from the Red Cow booked the 3 strippers for himself one night at his own house. He pushed the settee and chairs back to the wall. They did their show then got him!

The funniest stripper story Rob had seen was at Stoneygate Rugby Club. The usual set up of 2 strippers doing a show. One lad a loudmouth called Wez kept on touching the strippers and being disrespectful. One of the ladies got Wez to stand on a table and undid his belt. He continued showing off and he took his trousers and underpants down as he waved to his audience. In one movement the stripper rammed a 10-inch dildo straight up his arse! He did not see it coming, too busy waving. She didn't ease it in. One thrust, a great shot, only 2 inches stuck out at the bottom. He stood there motionless with a confused expression of surprise and pain on his face. Two strange things happened to him. He got a huge hardon! That he couldn't control, and he shit himself!

The mist cleared and Vicky was gone. 'Fucking amazing '. Dayle said.

The music got the mood back and once again the club was bouncing. The DJ had the bright idea of asking where people were from over the P.A. 'Anyone from Leeds, Sheffield, Derby, Leicester?' In turn groups would shout back from the crowd. The DJ must have known who had what holiday fortnights. When the DJ asked, 'who's from Derby?' Steve would viciously shout out 'Sheep shaggers!' hoping to entice a fight. Local rivalries are so tribal, it might be traced back to the Elizabethan Parish poor laws, but accents probably suggest that the tribal belonging goes back much further. Every time there's a change in the landscape, river, hills, moor, forest, there is a change in the accent.

This tribal rivalry was to show its face later. The lads had a great night and laugh in Top of The Pops. Outside they could not remember their way back so decided to get a cab. Rob waved a taxi and it pulled up. Rob opened the passenger door but heard arguing behind him, so he turned around.

'That's our fucking taxi'. A lad who Rob had never seen before said to Dez.

'How's it your taxi, he's just waved it down?' Steve replied.

The lad was with 3 mates. The taxi sped off.

'It's no one's now'. Rob said.

The lad turned to Rob and must have heard his East Midland's accent.

'Where you from?' he demanded.

'Leicester', Dayle replied.

'We are Fucking Forest ', the lad said holding his arms wide apart as an invitation to fight.

Rob only punched him once but it so hard that not only did his Citizen Watch fly off his wrist the Forest lad fell to the floor and Steve stuck the boot in, thud, thud, thud.

Boon nutted his mate with the blonde flick head with a squelching noise and he held his face in his hands, and the third ran off. Rob walked up to the lad on the floor 'You fucking wanker, I'm on mi 'olidays'.

Chapter 11- The End of Week 1

The food and the attitude of the staff in the Wishing Well was wearing thin within the group. They decided to eat in the Spanish restaurant opposite. It had the obligatory vinyl tablecloths, but this had a menu with pictures of the food in plastic covers as a menu. The waiter couldn't speak English, so Rob pointed at the Chicken Curry but then changed his mind and pointed at the mixed grill. Steve ordered the half roast chicken.

When Rob's meal came it was a chicken curry with a mixed grill on the top! 'This is the best meal, ever'. Rob said with glee.

Steve's meal was a chicken from the rotisserie with chips and salad. It had an olive oil dressing. Steve thought it was grease and fat and was disgusted and repeatedly punched his chicken. Each time he punched the carcass the white meat squeezed between his fingers. He didn't stop until he had putrefied and pummelled it.

On the way back to the apartment the lads walked along the promenade and as usual families were out enjoying the fading sun and sunset and promenading. Steve had small Nike nylon running shorts on and he was bragging about having the shits and his great cheek control. Then it happened. He stopped dead and brown watery liquid exploded down his bare legs through each leg of his shorts. It just kept coming and coming! It pebble dashed his legs and splattered the coloured paving stones. Families gasped in disgust. Steve ran into the sea.

The next evening the lads decided to try the English Chippie. The restaurant had a traditional English chip fryer and counter and the lads ordered sausage, chips and Pukka Pie and Chips. The husband and wife team who owned the restaurant were having the biggest row with each other behind the counter which continued through the ordering and eating of the meal. Boon said' Kin hell, do all the Brit's who own bars and businesses over here, bull and cow all the time?'

The meal was once again soured by the owner's bitterness. All was not ruined the lads decided to play football on the beach. They had left the ball in the apartment so Steve said that he would buy a cheap one from the beach shop. Steve went into the shop, bought a ball, walked out of the shop and then decided to boot it at the shop window! The group played football on the beach for half an hour and Rob commentated and pretended to be Gary Lineker.

The next day the gang decided to hire scooters for a day. They went to the hire shop and all hired Honda Melody's of different colours. They sped off into the Spanish countryside and up the hills behind the apartments. They didn't wear helmets and hooted and hollered and began re-enacting Quadrophenia, quoting lines from the film. Steve loved it and he was out of control. Back in the town he rode his scooter into amusement arcades. Dayle, Dez and Boon were having lunch in the Spanish Restaurant, Steve rode his scooter into the restaurant and up to the table! He rode it to the bar in the Beachcomber!

The lads were pleased when they had to return them for Steve's own safety!

Steve had the scooter bug. One-night Rob and Boon were sat in Kentucky Fried Chicken having a sobering meal about 1 AM so that they could line their stomachs to continue drinking. They looked out of the window and Steve was running down the side street pushing a Vespa! The Police were chasing him and whacking around the back of the legs and torso with their batons. Steve let go of the scooter and carried on running and the Police carried on hitting his legs and back before stopping. Rob and Boon rushed out of KFC and shouted Steve who was now walking. When they caught up with him, he made no reference to what had just happened!

Rob and Boon thought did they really see it?

Dayle's sunburn had eased by the end of the first week and he decided to buy some foam bath and have a soak in the tub. He filled his bath with bubbles and was just about ready to lock the door when Steve begged Dayle to nip for a week before he got in.

'Struth Steve, be quick'.

'Okay, Okay mate, two minutes.

Dayle finally locked the door and got into his bath. All was quiet, for two minutes then.

'Agghhhhh aghhhhh aghhhh Steve you dirty get, aghhhh, get it out!'

'What's wrong mate? I'll get it, let me in'. Dayle let him in and Steve went to the bubbles. 'It's like catching a goldfish mate'. Steve said with his hands in the water.

Un be known to Dayle, Steve had defecated in Dayle's bath and the brown fish had been hidden underneath the bubbles. A brown stealth submarine waiting for Dayle.

Steve's latest trick was buying a goldfish from the pet shop near the Geordie Bar and then tipping it into neat vodka and necking it! He said, 'I like the flappy feel down my neck!'

Week one soon turned into week two and it was going to be a holiday of two halves in terms of romance and violence.

Chapter 12 A Bad Day

The week began badly. For Dayle from the second day Dez had put some of his Sister's hair removal cream into Dayle's white Head and Shoulder's bottle of shampoo. His hair did not fall out completely but instead after every wash clumps would come out at a time, leaving Dayle looking like a mangey dog.

There was an atmosphere in the apartment and although Reuben, Rob's friend had once famously said' I'd much sooner live with a bloke than a split arse', the group had grown complacent and tetchy with each other.

Dez woke up and accused everyone of stealing his money from the table then accusing Steve that he had to pay for the free drink in the 2 for 1offer as Dez had paid. Steve had the mardies because Rob had put the glass coffee table over his head when he was asleep, so he was not sick on his mate's head again. Steve woke up and banged his head on the glass. Steve had died the concrete down the outside of the balcony light brown with his nightly spews.

Every night the workers handed out flyers for the Papa Whiskey Club. It was pay one price and eat and drink all you can. They decided to give it a go.

They had a few beers in the old town first, which is quaint and quintessentially Spanish compared to the modern high rise. The lads managed to end up in a Loyalist bar and once again were totally unaware of sectarian ideology. Coming from Middle England they never had any dealings with it. The closest Rob came to religion was telling his Mam when he was five, he didn't want to be a Cat lick as the Flannagan's across the road had to go to church on a Sunday dressed in shirt and ties.

Rob could remember having to leave the Co-op Department Store on High Street in the 1970's because of IRA hoaxed bomb threats but he never really understood. Rob's national pride was a personal pride. Steve and Rob had an altercation with two large Welsh girls in the afternoon. They were drunk and singing anti-English songs. Rob spoke up 'Why are you singing that we are all British?'

'We're not we are Welsh! Bread of Heaven, Bread of Heaven feed me 'till I want no moreeee'.

Rob had read that Leicester came from the word Leer which means Welsh. So, he was daft enough to tell the drunks this. Their reply was racist abuse about Leicester, which Rob took offence to and stop talking to the two horrors. Steve began signing the Gareth Edwards song!

'Gareth Edwards fucks his mother, Gareth Edwards Fucks his brother, all the Welsh they fuck each other, Fuck off back to Wales'.

The horrors went ballistic and threw a glass from a nearby table at Steve, who in turn threw one back. Rob had to hold him back 'What's that on your t-shirt your Welsh retard, Vera Moda? You dress like a tramp'. It was a big scene on the main road of the promenade now, Rob knew they had to scarper. This ridiculous xenophobic argument was drawing a crowd. The whole British argument was a farce. The English are a mongrel race, invasions of Celts, Romans, Angles, Saxons, Jutes, Vikings and Normans all settling and interbreeding makes the English truly mixed race even the name Anglish [Land of the Angles from Germany and Denmark] and the Anglo hyphen Saxon

name[from Saxony, Germany].
Xenophobia and racism make no sense.

After the furore the lads chilled on the balcony of the apartment. There was a couple in Spaghetti Western Bay making love, so Steve hurled oranges and apples from the fruit bowl trying to hit them from 19 floors up. The couple's shouts were inaudible as were their gestures unreadable.

The lads got ready for Papa Whiskey but decided to have a few happy hour drinks in the Square first. Boon wasn't there as he had pulled a girl from Essex. She was a very attractive dark-skinned girl called Jen, far too good looking for Boon. She was a journalism student at the University of Canterbury. Rob had lips on with her mate last night, but the lads said that she looked like Velma Dinkley from Scooby Doo and wound him up all day.

Boon was virtually living at her apartment and Jen was besotted by him. Boon was his usual, moody self and last night when he was sleeping, she smeared Nutella on him and was going to lick it off. Boon opened one eye and looked down at her and said, 'You can get that off'.

After the usual happy hour and a Wishing well beige tea the lads headed off to Papa Whiskey, paid their entrance fee and went downstairs. It was rubbish. The club was empty. The free drink was a turquoise blue mouthwash in glass jugs. Beer had to be paid for. The food trolley came out. Fish paste sandwiches,

Egg sandwiches. Rob said to' Dez, who on Earth makes fish cobs?' Rob remembered as a young boy going to Karen Carr's birthday party. He would have been five or six years old. The Co-op juice was always too strong, and her Mam had made fish paste and egg and cress sarnies. Why? Kids love them! Not.

Rob and Steve felt cheated and after eating as much as they could, they had a food fight and left. Dez and Dayle stopped. Back at the apartment Steve and Rob leant over the balcony and threw knives and forks at the dustbin men 19 floors below. The lads then went to bed.

Rob had no idea how long he'd been asleep but the banging repeatedly on the door woke him up. He thought it was Dez and Dayle and got up in his underpants. As he opened the door two Policemen burst in and in the darken room got Rob in an arm lock against the wall. They spoke in Spanish, one of them waved a knife and fork.

Voltairean good luck appeared again. At that very moment the Scot's door flew open at the other end of the small landing. Music blaring and all lit up. The Scot's were shouting and smashing their beds up throwing pine bed slats across the room. The Police immediately let go of Rob and dashed to the Scot's room of mayhem. The Police also must have thought that it was the Scot's who threw the cutlery as Rob was in his scants and the room was in darkness. Steve appeared from his balcony 'What's up mate?'.

Shortly Dez and Dayle appeared back arguing. 'Dez we need to get Rob and Steve and go back and get 'em.'

'Get who Dayle? No one got you ya muppet, you just ran off like a rare ass rabbit'.

'What's this then?' Dayle pulled up his linen shirt to reveal scrapes and scuffs on his back.

'Ha, what did they do? Give you a chicken run Dayle?'

'What's the craic?' Rob asked.

Dayle tried to talk but Dez butted in 'After you losers left, some Spicks came up to us outside. God knows what they were saying but I think it's cos we were chucking food about they were shouting on. Dayle just did one, he was like Daly

Thompson across the road and he fell hurdling the central reservation on the dual cabbage way. He's trying to say that they got him.'

'Did they get you? Rob replied.

'Yes, don't listen to him'. Dayle pleaded.

'Let's all go to kip lads eh. It's been a rank day'. Rob put his arm round Dayle's shoulder. 'C'mon Rocky, bedtime'.

Chapter 13 A Holiday of Two Halves

The next day was another clear blue day and Rob had been down the shop and bought bacon, eggs and sausage. He began cooking and Steve appeared from his balcony.

'Fresh mate?' Rob asked and Steve affirmed. The lads rose one by one and after the full English, the mood was restored. Rob suggested all day drinking [which was still illegal in England]. Upon Rob's suggestion the group burst into song to the tune of the Pet Shop Boy's, Domino Dancing.' All day, all day, all day drinking'.

It was another glorious Southern Spanish afternoon and the lads headed along the Promenade to a large and loud bar. Male Stripper by Man Parish boomed out the bar, across the golden beach and corrupted the still aquamarine sea.

The bar was rammed, and it took a while to get through the crowd in the gloom to the central, circumlunar bar with its

DJ booth inside. Boon and Jen were inside already standing with another girl. Dez and Steve went over whilst Rob and Dayle went to the bar. They got four bottles of Cruz Campo Beer and returned. Dez whispered in Rob's ear 'That's Velma mate, she looks hot without her bins on'.

Rob agreed and went to talk to her. It was her and Jen's last day and it was obvious that she'd made the effort for Rob. However, Rob had made the effort for himself with a Fila BJ polo shirt and matching Fila Tennis shorts.

The group were in good spirits, smiles all round. Then the music suddenly stopped. The whole bar turned around, maybe a hundred souls stared at the bar. A muscular blonde-haired man of around 21 years wearing Stone Island shorts and an Armani T-shirt was standing on the bar. He had a microphone in hand and began to speak.

'Can I have everyone's attention? There's a new Sheriff in town!' And with that he got down from the bar and Blue Monday by New Order began to play. The lads all looked at each other 'Was that Burchy?' Rob said.

'Kin 'ell it is, what's that nutter doing here?' said Boon. Burchy was from Leicester and part of the Leicester Forest East/ Red Cow crowd. He was wealthy but loved a good time. He was a few years older than Steve and Rob and they had gone to his 21st Birthday Party at the posh Peacock Alley a few Sunday nights ago. Burchy came across and he was all hugs and kisses. He sucked Rob's face and said, 'Hey the Stu Henson, beater upper'. Referring to a fight that Rob had with someone that Burchy knew. Along with Burchy was a lad from Braunstone known simply as Mad Ricky. He was short and stocky and game for a fight with anyone. He had Rick tattooed upon his neck.

Mad Ricky goosed any girl that walked past and usually pointed to the person next to him to blame them. A man dressed in a clown costume walked into the bar to sell roses and Ricky event commented to him 'Suppose you think ya funny?'

It was a great afternoon; the vibe was good and buoyant, and the group laughed. The intention was to carry on around the Square Bars. Boon said he was going for some scran with Jen and Rob and Velma joined them. The four of them walked along the promenade in the golden sunlight that cast dancing long grey shadows.

Velma leant over to Rob as they walked hand in hand and said, 'I need to pack, do you fancy walking me back rather than going for tea?' Rob agreed and the couple left Boon and Jen to their romantic last supper. They walked giggling and stopping for the odd kiss and enjoying each other's company for the last time. She repeatedly asked Rob Coyly if he will come up and see her. She phrased it many ways before pleading with him to visit. They reached the foyer of her apartments was marble, echoey and cold. They kissed Rob felt her breasts and hard nipples, he kissed her neck and felt her breathing change. Le petite morte. He had his hand up her skirt and into her cotton knickers. She stopped him.

'Not here, upstairs. Have you any protection?'

Rob replied, 'Why who's up there?'

'No, you idiot, condoms?' Rob shrugged and shook his head. That was it. The moment was lost. Velma gave Rob her number written on a nice post it pads and gave him one last tearful hug and kiss and then they parted. After leaving the apartment block with a semi on Rob scrunched up and threw the number away. Rob was fickle he liked girls for their clothes or haircut or eyeliner. If they changed them, he often went off them.

Burchy, Dayle, Ricky and Dez had gone to a brothel on the outskirts of town and returned to the Beachcomber Bar with its huge red and green neon palm tree sign outside. Rob headed towards it but met a middle-aged woman halfway across the square.

Five minutes later Rob was behind the pedalos on the beach and she was semi naked in her gold silky knickers sucking Rob off! After the deed was done, she said, 'My husband would never do this'.

Rob walked back to the alluring lights of the Beachcomber Bar and ordered a Brandy and Coke and 2 arrived, it was happy hour. Rob saw Dez and Burchy et al sitting down. Rob went over all smiles and shook hands with them. Rob took his seat next to a blonde girl. Rob never, ever thought that he was attractive but fuelled by his success tonight and Brandy and Cokes he kissed the girl without warning, and she kissed him back! Within ten minutes he was walking her back to her apartment and she was inviting him to Accrington!

Boon had left Jen and was walking alone. The night was over, and he was making his way back to the apartments. He walked past a worker girl who was sitting on the Beachcomber Wall. 'Had fun tonight? Where you been?' she asked.

'Been out all day, you know how it is?'. Boon was cool, oozed confidence and danger and well dressed.

'How about you show me how it is? I'm in room 247 give it five minutes and if I'm not down, come up', she said.

Boon gave it five and within five he was shagging like Michael Douglas against the patio doors.

Rob left the Scouse girl and headed back as he walked past the Silver Dollar Bar, he could see Steve at the bar. Rob walked in. There was no music on. The DJ looked up' Rob thank fuck you're here, what the fuck have you got on? You been playing tennis? Take Steve away mate will you he keeps on telling me the same joke about a cyclops in Burtons and the same rap'.

Pedro smiled on paternally and Steve began' A knife, a fork, that's the way you spell New York.2001 Nuclear bomb, mushrooms in the air, mushrooms everywhere, I'm the Brauny Frith Bomber and I'm faster and bolder'.

Rob said 'C'mon mate home time, smell my fingers, and with that he put his two forefingers up to Steve's nose.

On the way home, Rob said 'watch this', and battered a road sign around the pole with the side of his hand. Steve not to be beaten stuck his fist through a hotel light.

Rob looked at it, he could see the bones and the white tendons twitching. He said, 'Steve you need to get that sorted mate'.

Steve refused and Dez appeared up the sloping road. Dez was mangled drunk. Rob explained what had happened and Dez asked for a look and Steve obliged. Dez immediately spat a greeny spit into the wound and started his Muttley laugh.

Rob thought the best thing to do was to see Pedro. Being a father figure, he put the boys in a cab and ordered the Spanish driver to take them to the clinic. The Clinic was in darkness, but life stirred when Rob pressed the bell. An attractive Spanish nurse answered the robust wooden door and the boys entered the fluorescent lit clinic. Steve was stitched up by a Doctor Rob sorted out the bill with the nurse.

The walk back took them across wasteland and a disused fair. Some Spanish lads approached and spoke in Spanish and offered the boys drugs, Rob declined and shook hands with the Spaniards who realised that Steve and Rob were working class lads like themselves. Panniaro.

Chapter 13 Take Me Back to Dear Old Blighty

The last day was a pain. Dayle was euphoric as he had grown homesick. He was the youngest of the group, youngest of his family and the most vulnerable. Steve too was high as kite; he was determined to make the most of his last day and sprang about outside the apartment taking photos as he had not taken any before on the trip.

They had to be out of the apartment by midday, but their flight was not until the Eleven O'clock at night. It was a day hanging around the Sol Pellicanos' pool as that's where they had to store their cases and were being picked up from by the transfer coach. It was a large hotel and quite plush from what the lads had experienced. They almost felt out of place. Rob hated the feeling that made him feel condescended upon. How he felt middle class people looked down upon the working classes. The worst were those who had come from Council estate backgrounds but made it into the echelons of the private estate and sales reps' jobs. No way were they going back, and they had to hide their origins. Rob remembers sitting on a train to go to Sheffield and two wannabe middle class ladies sitting near him tried to out posh each other. They were in their 40s and spoke of the Young Farmers parties they had been to, holidays to Gites in France and Prague.

They were full of it and one of them even had a Brompton fold up bike. They were ugly too but tried to make themselves interesting with coloured Doc Martin's with bright laces, baggy jeans, dayglo tights and horrible striped crusty rainbow woolly jumpers. Rob hated them. He hated how they made him feel. He wanted to drop bombs on Last Night of the Proms.

The Geordies had a word for these types of people. They called them 'Rahs'. The name comes from their accents 'RAH, RAH'. They lived-in middle-class areas like Jesmond or Tynemouth, wore ripped jeans and flip flops, had messy hair. Spoke without a trace of a Geordie accent but had jobs in coffee shops, never bee to university, toothickforuniversity, looked after by their banker or art dealing parents.

The lads splashed out and went to Burger King for their dinner. They had never seen one before. Leicester had only just got a MacDonald's near the Clock Tower, where the Leicester way shop had been before, and selling things like Elvis Mirrors and pin badges. The name Whopper made the lads laugh as euphemism. Steve said, 'The burgers from Leftley's Old Man's Van outside Irish are better', he wizzes in the onions'.

The feeling was one of anti-climax like Christmas Day night or the morning after a top night out with your mates. The lads were too young for beer fear, but they had started to realise that the Saturday Night conversations were Charlatans to the Sunday mornings.

The coach came with the same sour faced representative and they did relatively fewer pick-ups than drop offs. The lads gawped jealously out of the windows at the clip clop of white high heels and the people on the streets going to the neon lit bars beckoning them in like the faithful to the bell or the sinners into the alluring Devil's arms. Dusk was falling into darkness and the coach headed for Alicante Airport and the high rise was left behind and the shadows of the huge wooden bull's silhouetted against the night.

In the departure lounge the lads had a welcome surprise. Ricky and Burchy were there! They were steaming and on the same flight! Ricky and Burchy drank in the Falcon in Braunstone. Rob went in there once to see Steve and Biffo and there was a guy in there with a Boa Constrictor around his neck and another guy stubbed his fag out on the snake's head!

'Lads, Lads, lads. Burchy's shout was so loud. He ran over to Boon and jumped on him knocking him over and into a drinks machine. He then kissed his cheek. They had been on the drink for two days solid and were worse for wear. Burchy had been warned twice by customer service agents.

Once again, the group were given the worst seats at the back of the plane. It sped down the tarmac leaving the twinkling lights of the Costa Blanca behind as they were cuddled into the dark abyss of the sky.

The Bing of the cabin crew free to go about their duties sounded and Ricky watched intently how one of the cabin crew announced using a telephone intercom system what the hot meal was.

It was some microwaved stodge made in some industrial kitchen by Puritan Maid in Dunstable. Steve hoped for the breakfast, but it was Beef Stroganoff or chicken chasseur.

The flight levelled off and the release seat belt sign pinged. The cabin crew went about their tedious business like playing in a dolls house with tiny cups and cans of coke. People queued for the toilets like they had never been to the toilet before [even though they left only twenty minutes ago].

The customer announcement system echoed into life 'This is the Captain speaking, Brace, Brace, we are going to crash'!

Time seemed to stand still but in retrospect things happened quickly. Rob looked to the front of the plane and the rows of customers were leaning forward with their heads in their laps and palms on the back of their heads.

Immediately there was another announcement. 'This is the real Captain speaking, ignore that last statement it was make by a drunken passenger'.

By Ricky! The cabin crew removed Ricky and took him to the front of the plane and two sat beside him for the rest of the flight. Further announcements were made asking customers to press the call button if they wanted to press charges against Ricky and finally when the plane landed at East Midland's Airport Ricky was escorted away by the Police and further Police came on the plane appealing for witness statements. Burchy joined his friend in the Police Van as he had been caught taking Champagne from the unguarded drinks trolley!

The smell of aviation fuel greeted the lad's nostrils when they got off the plane and didn't disappear until they were through customs. Dayle's Dad and Dez's sister were there to meet them.

Epilogue

The only thing one can be sure of in life is change. When you're young and the summers last a long time, winter seems years away. Plans to be friends forever and your siblings to be friends rarely pan out in the urban world.

The holiday was a watershed in the lives of the group. Dayle left the friendship group and began to mix with lads from his estate who he went to school with and enjoyed the safety of the mainstream and devoted his time at weekend trying to pull the ladies. His hair grew back.

Boon and Steve became closer and spent more time with the Leicester Forest East, Red Cow lads. They also went into business together as painter and decorators. Steve bought a 100 canisters of C.S gas from a lad in Nottingham and he accidently set them off all the time in his pockets in the Red Cow pub. They also took a young lad, Queenie under their wing and he ended up owning a bar in Majorca after working abroad with Boon in Tenerife. Boon was too cool for glass collecting and returned home, Queenie ended up with 3 successful bars and a Ferrari.

Dez got the girl next door pregnant and had a baby. He moved out and bought himself a house in the Newfoundpool area of Leicester. Sometimes on his way home from town Steve would break in and attack Dez in his balaclava with his cosh for a laugh. Dez began playing rugby for New Parks Old Boy's Rugby Club with Steve.

Rob's life changed dramatically. He was soon to realise what Prefab Sprout meant 'Some things hurt far much more than cars and girls. He spent more time with Miranda, and they booked a holiday to Jamaica and Florida which was the nail in the coffin for Steve and Rob's friendship, whom had planned a holiday. Rob had let Steve down, his most loyal friend.

Rob began going to the football again with Sooty and the Knighton part of the Baby Squad. Sooty was well-educated and middle class. He taught Rob about how showing labels was crass and introduced him to brands like Chevignon, Chipie and Boneville. The take aways stopped with Sooty as he insisted that money's better invested. Steve carried on having his Chicken Tikka Joe Frasier [Jal Friezi] he even ate them out of the carton walking home from town! A couple of years later Rob began spending his Saturday's egg chasing for Anstey Rugby Club with Stroudy, Reuben and Young Bryn.

 Rob took a job at the dairy with his Dad earning real money, but sadness was to enter his life and change everything when he arrived at work on morning to find his Dad dead. It was an awful experience for him especially when the Co-operative Dairy on Glenfield Road stopped production for the first time in 100 years whilst the workers doffed their caps to the coffin and Rob and his

Mam in the funeral Courtage. Rob felt empty inside, but his loyal friend Steve was there for him and reforged their friendship. Rob played the Charlatan's debut album, Some Friendly over and over again thinking of his Dad and whilst his Dad was gone, he always felt that he was close by. When he was in America Rob constantly dreamt of his Dad and the dreams were so real in the half light of the morning. The Chrysler car stereo seemed to play the same song to remind Rob, Love song by The Cure. Rob's Mam said that she could smell his Park drive fags sometimes in the house and sensed her husband there.

Everything was to change at the end of the 80s. Music moved from time served guitar-based musicians and polished commercial black artists to the DJ becoming king. The House music revolution starting with Marshall Jefferson, Steve Silk Hurley, Graham Park and Farley Jackmaster Funk; often playing in gay clubs. The only time the lads had ever been to a gay bar was when the once went into the Dover Castle Pub in Leicester in the mid-1980s when the lads called in for a look and were chased down the street after by Skinhead queer bashers! Rob started going to Street Life in Leicester, Venus and The Garage in Nottingham. The use of Chemical stimulants and their euphoric, loved up affects chimed the death knell for the football violence era. Even though Rob and his Forest friend Paul Hall were approached by some wannabe Baby Squad lads for a fight as later as 1995!

With the Yuppie years and more affluent society the class system became more blurred yet, it's not about money it's about stigma and culture. The Beckham's may have epitomised new money just as the Spencer's et al did in Tudor times buying up cheap monastery land. The nouveux riche might have big houses but they still had the style, culture and ultimately, stigma of the working class. People were more afraid of the stigma of the workhouse than going there. The stigma of the council estate is worse than living there.

All the troubles and tribulations of the working classes and the lads in this story can be traced back to the Forty Third of

Elizabeth and parish rivalries, beating of the bounds, persecution of paupers, Egyptians and Repeaters. Similarly, The 1834 Poor Law Act with its stigma of the Workhouse and their franchises, panopticons of paupers. Thatcher and her reverence of all things Victorian [except she omitted to understand their hatred of debt], The Right to Buy Scheme, Youth Training Schemes, and Privatisation buying shares in things that we already own. Every action has a reaction.

Printed in Great Britain
by Amazon